ILLUSTRATIONS

(*After Drawings by* THOMAS RUNCI-
MAN)

Publisher's Note

Purchase of this book entitles you to a free trial membership in the publisher's book club at www.rarebooksclub. com. (Time limited offer.) Simply enter the barcode number from the back cover onto the membership form on our home page. The book club entitles you to select from millions of books at no additional charge. You can also download a digital copy of this and related books to read on the go. Simply enter the title or subject onto the search form to find them.

Note: This is an historic book. Pages numbers, where present in the text, refer to the first edition of the book and may also be in indexes.

If you have any questions, could you please be so kind as to consult our Frequently Asked Questions page at www. rarebooksclub.com/faqs.cfm? You are also welcome to contact us there.

Publisher: General Books LLC™, Memphis, TN, USA, 2012. ISBN: 9781443220941.
Proofreading: pgdp.net

❖❖ ❖❖ ❖❖ ❖❖ ❖❖ ❖❖ ❖❖ ❖❖

WINDJAMMERS AND SEA TRAMPS

By

WALTER RUNCIMAN, Sen.

Author of "The Shellback's Progress in the Nineteenth Century."

**SECOND EDITION.
LONDON AND NEWCASTLE-ON-TYNE:
THE WALTER SCOTT
PUBLISHING CO., LTD.
NEW YORK: 3 EAST 14TH STREET.
1905.**

"THE —— RATS HAVE EATEN UP HOLLAND"

**THESE EXPERIENCES AND OPINIONS
OF THINGS NAVAL
NEW AND OLD
ARE DEDICATED
WITH EVERY SENTIMENT OF ESTEEM**

**TO
JOHN DENT AND WILLIAM MILBURN
AND TO THE MEMORY OF
E.H. WATTS**

PREFACE

"I went in at the hawse-hole and came out at the cabin window." It was thus that a certain North Country shipowner once summarised his career while addressing his fellow-townsmen on some public occasion now long past, and the sentence, giving forth the exact truth with all a sailor's delight in hyperbole, may well be taken to describe the earlier life-stages gone through by the author of this book. The experiences acquired in a field of operations, that includes all the seas and continents where commerce may move, live, and have its being, have enhanced in value and completed what came to him in his forecastle and quarter-deck times. He learned in his youth, from the lips of a race now extinct, what the nature and traditions of seamanship were before he and his contemporaries lived. He has seen that nature and those traditions change and die, whilst he and his generation came gradually under a new order of things, whose practical working he and they have tested in actual practice both on sea and land.

It is on this ground of experience that the author ventures to ask attention to his views in respect of the likeliest means to raise a desirable set of seamen in the English merchant navy. But he also ventures to hope that the historic incidents and characteristics of a class to which he is proud to belong, as set forth in this book, may cause it to be read with interest and charitable criticism. He claims no literary merit for it: indeed, he feels there may be found many defects in style and description that could be improved by a more skilful penman. But then it must be remembered that a sailor is here writing of sailors, and hence he gives the book to the public as it is, and hopes he has succeeded in making it interesting.

CHAPTER I

INTRODUCTORY

It was a bad day for Spain when Philip allowed the "Holy Office" to throw Thomas Seeley, the Bristol merchant, into a dungeon for knocking down a Spaniard who had uttered foul slanders against the Virgin Monarch of England. Philip did not heed the petition of the patriot's wife, of which he must have been cognisant. Elizabeth refused the commission Dorothy Seeley petitioned for, but, like a sensible lady, she allowed her subjects to initiate their own methods of revenge. Subsequent events show that she had no small share in the introduction of a policy that was ultimately to sweep the Spaniards off the seas, and give Britain the supremacy over all those demesnes. This was the beginning of a distinguished partnership composed of Messieurs John Hawkins and his kinsman Francis Drake, and of Elizabeth their Queen. Elizabeth did not openly avow herself one of the partners; she would have indignantly denied it had it been hinted at; yet it is pretty certain that the cruises of her faithful Hawkins and Drake substantially increased her wealth, while they diminished that of Spanish Philip and that of his subjects too. Long before the Armada appeared resplendent in English waters, commanded by that hopeless, blithering landlubber, the Duke of Medina Sidonia, who with other sons of Spain was sent forth to fight against Britain for "Christ and our Lady," there had been trained here a race of daredevil seamen who knew no fear, and who broke and vanquished what was reckoned, till then, the finest body of sailors in the whole world. That our sailors have maintained the reputation achieved in the destruction of the great Spanish Armada is sometimes disputed. I am one of those who trust that British seamen would be worthy of British traditions were they even now put to the test by some powerful invader. To suppose that the men who smothered the Armada, or those who broke the fleets of Spain and France at Trafalgar, were more courageous than those of our day would be found in similar circumstances, is arrant folly. In smaller things we can see the same sterling qualities shown by members of our Navy now as their forebears exhibited of old. The impressive yet half comic character of the religion that guided the lives of seamen during Drake's time has been faithfully handed down like an heirloom to the genuine old salt of our own time.

The great Admiral had inconsistencies of character, and conduct that would seem to live on in more or less elevated examples up till now. He conducted himself in regal style on his long voyages, dressing in an imposing way for dinner, during which he commanded fine music to be played—for at that day England was the home *par excellence* of music—and no food was eaten at his table until the blessing of the Almighty had been asked upon it, and "thanks" was solemnly offered ere rising. The Holy Sacrament was partaken by him with Doughty the Spanish spy. The latter, after being kissed by Drake, was then made to lay his head on the block, and thereafter no more was heard of him. Afterwards the Admiral gave forth a few discourses on the importance of unity and obedience, on the sin of spying into other people's affairs; and then proceeded, with becoming solemnity and in the names of God and the Icy Queen, to plunder Spanish ports and Spanish shipping. Drake believed he was by God's blessing carrying out a divinely governed destiny, and so perhaps he was; but it is difficult somewhat to reconcile his covetousness with his piety. But what is to be said of his Royal mistress whose crown and realm were saved to her by free sacrifices of blood and life on the part of thousands of single-minded men, whom the Royal Lady calmly allowed, after they had secured her safety and that of England, to starve in peace on Margate Sands? Times have changed. Were such reward to be meted to the sailors of to-day after some great period of storm, stress and national peril had been passed through by virtue of their prowess, the wrath of the nation might break forth and go near to sweep away such high-placed callousness for good and all.

The modern austere critic of the condition of the seamen of the mercantile marine is somewhat of an infliction. He slays the present-day sailor with virulent denunciation, and implores divine interposition to take us back to the good old days of Hawkins, Drake, Howard, Blake and the intrepid Nelson. He craves a resurrection of the combined heroism and piety of the sixteenth and the beginning of the nineteenth centuries. The seaman of those periods is, to his mind, a lost ideal. And without doubt the men trained and disciplined by Hawkins and Drake *were* the glory of Britain and the terror of other nationalities. Their seamanship and heroism were matchless. They had desperate work to do, and they did it with completeness and devotion. And the same credit may be given to the sailors of still later times under altered conditions. But Nelson's and Collingwood's men did great deeds in different ways from those of Hawkins and Drake. Both sets of seamen were brave and resourceful, but they were made use of differently, and were drafted from different sources. The latter were seamen and piratical rovers by choice, and warriors very often by necessity. They were willing, however, to combine piety, piracy, and sanguinary conflict in the effort to open out new avenues of commercial enterprise for the mutual benefit of themselves and the thrifty lady who sat upon the throne, and who showed no disinclination to receive her share of the booty valiantly acquired by her nautical partners.

The race of men which followed the Trans-Atlantic, Pacific, and Mexican buccaneers of Cadiz, San Juan and Armada fame has been different only in so far as transitional circumstances have made it so. Indeed, the period which elapsed from the time of the destruction of the Armada up to the end of the eighteenth and the beginning of the nineteenth century had evolved innumerable changes in modes of commerce which changed our seamen's characteristics as well. But although the circumstances of the sailors' avocation had changed, and they had to adapt themselves to new customs, there is no justification for the belief that the men of the sixteenth were any more capable or well behaved than those of the eighteenth and the beginning of the nineteenth centuries. Nor is it justifiable to assume that because of the rapid changes which have taken place during the last fifty years by the introduction of steamers, the seamen who man the steamers are inferior to those who, a generation before, manned sailing vessels, or who man what is left of sailing vessels now. The steamer seamen of to-day are mentally, physically and mechanically as competent to do the work they are engaged to do as were any previous race of seamen, and, taking them in the aggregate, they are better educated than their predecessors and quite as sober. Their discipline may not be all that could be desired, but that is not the fault of, nor need it even be considered a defect in, the seaman himself. It is a defect of the system they live under, the responsibility for which must rest with those whose duty it is to train them. It often happens that those who declaim so cynically against the shortcomings of the present-day sailor are incompetent to make a suitable selection of captains and officers who may be entrusted with the task of establishing proper discipline and training aboard their vessels. Very frequently the seamen are blamed when the captain and officers ought to be held responsible. If captains and officers are not trained properly in their graduating process themselves, and have not the natural ability to make up for that misfortune when given the opportunity of control, it is inevitable that disorder must follow. There are, however, exceptional cases where, for example, an officer may have been reared in a bad, disorderly school, and yet has become a capable disciplinarian. An instance of this kind seldom occurs; but the merchant service is all the richer for it when it does. It must not be supposed that I have any intention of defending the faults of our seamen. I merely desire that some of the responsibility for their faults and training should be laid on the shoulders of those critics who shriek unreasonably of their weaknesses, while they do nothing to improve matters. Many of these gentlemen complain of Jack's drunken, insubordinate habits, while they do not disapprove of putting temptation in his way. They complain of him not being proficient, and at the same time they refuse to undertake the task of efficient training. They cherish the memory of the good old times. They speak reverently of the period of flogging, of rotten and scanty food allowance, of perfidious press-gangs, and of corrupt bureaucratic tyranny that inflicted unspeakable torture on the seamen who manned our line of battleships at the beginning of the century—seamen who were, for the most part, pressed away from the merchant service.

In my boyhood days I often used to hear the old sailors who were fast closing their day of active service say that there were no sailors nowadays. They had all either been "drowned, killed, or had died at home and been decently buried." I was impressed in those days with the opinions of these vain old men, and thought how great in their profession they must have been. As a matter of fact, they were no better nor any worse than the men against whom a whimsical vanity caused them to inveigh. Many years have passed since I had the honour of sailing with them and many, if not all of them, may be long since dead; but I sometimes think of them as amongst the finest specimens of men that ever I was associated with. Their fine manhood towered over everything that was common or mean, in spite of their wayward talk.

CHAPTER II
PECULIAR AND UNEDUCATED

The average seaman of the middle of the nineteenth century, like his predecessor, was in many respects a cruel animal. To appearance he was void of every human feeling, and yet behind all the rugged savagery there was a big and generous heart. The fact is, this apparent or real callousness was the result of a system, pernicious in its influence, that caused the successive generations of seafaring men to swell with vanity if they could but acquire the reputation of being desperadoes; and this ambition was not an exclusive possession of those whose education had been deplorably neglected. It was proudly shared by some of the best educated men in the service. I do not wish it to be supposed, however, that many of them had more than a very ordinary elementary education; but be that as it may, they got along uncommonly well with the little they had. Mr. Forster's Educational Bill of 1870, together with Wesleyan Methodism, have done much to nullify that cultivation of ignorance, once the peculiar province of the squire and the parson. Amongst other influences, Board Schools have revolutionised (especially in the villages and seaport towns) a condition that was bordering on heathenism, and no class of workmen has benefited more than seamen by the propaganda which was established by that good Quaker who spent his best years in hard effort to make it possible that every English child, no matter how poor, should have an education.

At the time of the passing of the Education Act there were thousands of British lads who were absolutely illiterate (this does not apply so much to Scottish boys); and there were hundreds of master-mariners who could neither read nor write, and who had a genuine contempt for those who could. They held the notion that learning, as they called it, always carried with it nautical ignorance and general deterioration; and in some instances the old salts' opinions seemed amply borne out by palpable blunders in practical seamanship which were not uncommonly made when the theoretic seaman or navigator was at work. These shortcomings of the "learned" were never forgotten or forgiven by the practical though illiterate seamen.

Until well into the 'fifties the northeast coast collier brigs and schooners were usually commanded by this type of illiterates, and innumerable stories might be told of their strange methods and grotesque beliefs. The following is a fair example. The London trade once became congested with tonnage, and a demand sprang up for Holland, whereupon a well-known brig was chartered for Rotterdam. She had been so long employed running along the coast with the land aboard that the charts became entirely neglected. When the time came to say farewell there was more than ordinary affection displayed by the relatives of the crew whose destiny it was to penetrate what they conceived to be the mysteries of an unexplored East. There were not a few females who regarded the undertaking as eminently heroic. With characteristic carelessness the trim craft was rollicked along the Yorkshire coast until abreast of Flamborough Head, when it became necessary to take a departure and shape a course for Rotterdam. She scampered along at the rate of six to seven knots an hour amid much anxiety among the crew, for a growing terror had possessed the captain and his mate as they neared the unknown dangers that were ahead of them. The captain went below and had begun to unroll the chart which indicated the approaches to his destination, when he became horrorstruck, and rushing up the cabin stairs called out, "All hands on deck! Hard, a port!" The mate excitedly asked, "What's the matter?" "The mat-

ter?" said the infuriated and panic-stricken skipper, "Why the b——y rats have eaten Holland! There is nee Rotterdam for us, mister, *this* voyage." But in spite of a misfortune which seemed serious, the mate prevailed upon this distinguished person to allow *him* to have a share in the navigation, with the result that the vessel reached the haven to which she was bound without any mishap whatever.

It was not unusual for those old-time brigs, when bound to the North in ballast, to be blown off the land by strong westerly gales, and these occasions were dreaded by the coasting commander whose geographical knowledge was so limited that when he found himself drifting into the German Ocean beyond the sight of land, his resources became too heavily taxed, and perplexity prevailed. It was on one of those occasions that a skipper, after many days of boisterous drifting, remarked to his mate, "I wish our wives knew where we are this terrible night!"

"Yes," replied the shrewd officer, with comic candour; "and I wish to heaven we knew where we are ourselves!"

Such was the almost opaque ignorance, in spite of which a very large carrying trade was successfully kept going for generations.

The writing of the old-time skipper was so atrocious that it brought much bad language into the world. One gentleman used to say that his captain's letters used to go all over the country before they fell into his hands, and when they did, they were covered over with "try here" and "try there." Their manners, too, were aboriginal; and they spoke with an accent which was terrible. They rarely expressed themselves in a way that would indicate excessive purity of character. They thought it beneath the dignity of a man to be of any other profession than that of a sailor. They disdained showing soft emotion, and if they shook hands it was done in an apologetic way. The gospel of pity did not enter into their creed. Learning, as they called it, was a bewilderment to them; and yet some of those eccentric,

half-savage beings could be entrusted with valuable property, and the negotiation of business involving most intricate handling. Sometimes in the settlement of knotty questions they used their own peculiar persuasiveness, and if that was not convincing, they indicated the possibility of physical force—which was usually effectual, especially with Levantines. Here is an instance: one of the latter plethoric gentlemen, with an air of aggrieved virtue, accused a captain of unreasonableness in asking him to pay up some cash which was "obviously an overcharge." The skipper in his rugged way demanded the money and the clearance of his vessel. The gentlemen who at this time inhabited the banks of the Danube could not be made to part with money without some strong reasons for doing so. The Titanic and renowned captain, having exhausted a vocabulary that was awful to listen to, proceeded to lock the office door on the inside. That having been satisfactorily done, he proceeded to unrobe himself of an article of apparel; which movement, under certain conditions, is always suggestive of coming trouble. The quick brain of the Levantine gentleman saw in the bellicose attitude assumed possibilities of great bodily harm and suffering to himself; on which he became effusively apologetic, and declaimed with vigorous gesticulation against the carelessness of his "account clerk who had committed a glaring error, such as justified his immediate dismissal!" That stalwart hero of many rights had not appealed in vain. He got his money and his clearance, and made a well-chosen and impressive little speech on the wisdom of honest dealing. His convert for the time being became much affected, declaring that he had never met with a gentleman whose words had made such a strange impression on him!

This then was the kind of creature who wrought into its present shapes and aspects England's Mercantile Marine. In carrying out his destiny he lashed about him with something of the elemental aimlessness of his mother the sea. The next chapter will show how the captain of to-day grew up and, literally, got licked into his present form at the rough and cruel hands of the old-time skipper.

CHAPTER III

A CABIN-BOY'S START AT SEA

During recent years I have had the opportunity of listening to many speeches on nautical subjects. Some of them have not only been instructive but interesting, inasmuch as they have often enabled me to get a glimpse into the layman's manner of thinking on these questions. It invariably happens, however, that gentlemen, in their zeal to display maritime knowledge, commit the error of dealing with a phase of it that carries them into deep water; their vocabulary becomes exhausted, and they speedily breathe their last in the oft-repeated tale that the "old-fashioned sailor is an extinct creature," and, judging from the earnest vehemence that is thrown into it, they convey the impression that their dictum is to be understood as emphatically original. Well, I will let that go, and will merely observe how distressingly superficial the knowledge is as to the rearing, training, and treatment which enabled those veterans to become envied heroes to us of the present day. Much entered into their lives that might be usefully emulated by the seamen of our own time. Their unquestionable skill and hardihood were acquired by a system of training that would have out-matched the severity of the Spartan, and they endured it with Spartan equanimity. A spasmodic growl was the only symptom of a rebellious spirit. The maritime historian who undertakes to write accurately the history of this strange society of men will find it a strain on the imagination to do them all the justice they deserve. Their lives were illuminated with all that is manly and heroic and skilful. They had no thought of cruelty, and yet they were very cruel—that is, if they are to be judged by the standard of the present age; but in this let us pass sentence on them with moderation, and even with indulgence. The magnitude of the deeds they were accustomed to perform can never be fully estimated now, and these

should excuse to some extent many of their clumsy and misguided modes of operation. It must not be supposed that all these men were afflicted by a demoniac spirit. It was their training that blanketed the sympathetic side of them, until they unconsciously acquired all the peremptory disposition of Oriental tyrants. But the stories I am about to relate of childlife aboard ship will show how difficult it is entirely to pardon or excuse them. The blood runs chilly at the thought of it, and you feel your mind becoming impregnated with the spirit of murder.

No personage ever attracted so much attention and sympathy outside the precincts of his contracted though varied sphere of labour as the cabin-boy who served aboard the old sailing brigs, schooners, and barques, and I must plead guilty to having a sentimental regret that the romance was destroyed through this attractive personality being superseded by another, with the somewhat unattractive title of "cook and steward." The story of how poor boys of the beginning and middle of the century and right up to the latter part of the 'sixties started sea-life is always romantic, often sensational, and ever pathetic. They were usually the sons of poor parents living for the most part in obscure villages or small towns bordering on the sea, which sea blazed into their minds aspirations to get aboard some one of the numerous vessels that passed their homes one way or the other all day long. The notion of becoming anything but sailors never entered their heads, and the parents were usually proud of this ambition, and quite ready to allow their offspring to launch out into the world while they were yet little more than children. It very frequently happened, however, that boys left their homes unknown to their families, and tramped to the nearest seaport with the object of engaging themselves aboard ship, and they nearly always found some skipper or owner to take them. Swarms of Scotch and Norfolk boys were attracted to the Northumberland ports by the higher rate of wages. Many of them had to tramp it all the long way from home,

and quite a large number of them became important factors in the shipping trade of the district. It was a frequent occurrence to see a poor child-boy passing through the village where I was brought up, on his way from Scotland to Blyth, or the Tyne, his feet covered with sores, and carrying a small bundle containing a shirt, a pair of stockings, and flannel pants. This was his entire outfit. My mother never knowingly allowed any of these poor little wanderers to pass without bringing them to our home. They were promptly supplied with bread and milk while the big tub was got ready so that they might be bathed. They were then provided with night clothing and put to bed while she had their own clothes washed, and mended if need be (they always required washing); they were then sent on their journey with many petitions to God for their safety and welfare. Some of the villagers were curious to know why this gratuitous hospitality was given to unknown passers-by, and my mother satisfied their curiosity by pointing to her own children, and remarking, "Don't we live within the sound of the sea? and I wish to do by these poor children that which I should like some one to do by mine if it ever should come to pass that they need it." Little did she suspect when these words were uttered that one of her own sons was so soon to be travelling in an opposite direction in quest of a cabin-boy's berth.

One of the most touching memories of sweetness comes to me now. It was a chill winter afternoon; a little boy stood out on the common fronting our house; the customary bundle was under his arm, and he was singing in a sweet treble these words, with a strong Scotch accent:—

"A beggar man came over the lea
Wi' many a story to tell unto me.
'I'm asking for some charitie,
Can ye lodge a beggar man?'"

The charm of his silken, childish voice quickly attracted attention. He was put through the usual catechism by my parents, and this being satisfactory, he fell into my mother's hands to undergo the customary feeding and bathing operations. One of the questions my father put to him was why he sang "The beggar man." He said they told him at home that he could sing well, and as he had learnt this song he thought it might serve the purpose of bringing him succour, as he was very tired and very hungry. He was the son of a peasant farmer on the outskirts of Kirkaldy in the Firth of Forth, and had walked the whole distance, his object being to apprentice himself to some shipowner. This he succeeded in doing; and many years after, when he had worked his way into a position, he made himself known to me by recalling the occasion when he sang his way into our home.

By the seaside on the coast of Northumberland, there stands one of the prettiest little villages in all England. Tacked on to the north and south end of it there are two stretches of sand unequalled in their clear glossy beauty. It was from this spot that a boy of twelve summers, smitten with a craze for the sea, secretly left his home one December morning at three o'clock with the object of becoming a sailor. He made his way to the beach, walked to a seaport, and after much persuasive eloquence in which he recklessly pledged himself to impossible undertakings, the negotiations were ratified by his being told by a burly skipper of the old school that though he was very small, yet seeing he exhibited such eagerness for the fray, he would look over that, to which the seaman in embryo promptly replied, "But, sir, I will grow bigger." And the weather-beaten old mariner responded, "I hope you will; but mind, you'll have to work."

The poor child, fearful lest any hitch should come in the way, assured him that he could work very hard, and that he could run up aloft, as he had tried it aboard a schooner which came once a year to his home with coals for the squire. He was anxious that his accomplishments should be tested without delay. His future commander interjected that he would sign his indentures the following week, which was done, after communication with the boy's family; and he proceeded aboard with his kit

made up of the following articles. I give this, as it may be useful to parents who have boys going to sea:—

1 Box.
1 Go-ashore suit.
2 Suits of working clothes.
1 Suit of oilskins.
1 Pair of sea-boots.
1 Pair of shoes.
3 Changes of flannels.
6 Pairs of stockings.
2 Mufflers.
4 Towels.
3 Coloured flannel shirts.
1 Bar of soap.
6 Collars, 2 neckties.
2 Pillow-slips.
1 Bed and full set of bedding.
2 Caps.
1 Canvas bag.
1 Ditty bag well stored with needles, thread,
buttons, thimble, worsted to darn stockings, and
cloth to patch worn or torn clothes.

This outfit is quite ample, and is more than double what some poor boys had to start life with; indeed, scores of them had to depend on what their first quarter's wages would provide for them. In many country homes boys were taught, as this boy was, sewing, darning, and even washing. The knowledge of it cannot eat anything, and it is immensely useful to have it. This might be commended to present-day parents in town and country who have lads to send out into the world. There is no loss of dignity in being able to do something for yourself in the event of being too poor to pay for having it done for you. A more exhilarating sight could not be witnessed than that of sailors and sailor boys sitting sewing their clothes or doing their week's washing.

TARRING THE MAINMAST STAY

I have said the initial training and experiences of a cabin-boy were not only harsh but oft-times brutal. No allowance was made for his tender years. The gospel of pity did not enter into the lives of either the captains, officers, or men. He was expected to learn without being taught, and if he did not come up to

their standard of intelligence, his poor little body was made to suffer for it. This happened more or less to every boy, and our new recruit was not made an exception. He was given to understand that certain duties devolved upon him. The language perplexed his little brain. He had heard nothing like it before, but he determined to avail himself of every opportunity of learning. His inquisitiveness was a trouble to the men; they rebuked him for bothering them; but by steady plodding he began to learn the names of the multiplicity of ropes, and the different things he would have to do when the vessel put to sea. He was ordered to have the side lights trimmed ready for lighting, the day before sailing (a very wise precaution which should always be adhered to). This was done, and although the wee laddie had only been four days amidst a whirl of things that were strange to him, he seemed to think that he had acquired sufficient knowledge to justify him in believing that he had mastered the situation. He wrote home a detailed account of his doings, and complicated matters by using phrases that were not commonly heard or understood in quiet villages far away from the hum of seaports. The family were sent into consternation by the description of his climbing experiences, and an extra petition for his safe-keeping was offered up when the time for family devotions came. No more was heard of him for many months. His experiences had become more real and fuller ere the next letter came. On the fifth day after he had embarked the tug came alongside, the tow-rope was handed aboard, and the vessel towed out of dock to sea. Night was coming on, and the boy was ordered to light the side lamps; he was in the act of doing this when the pitching of the vessel afflicted him with strange sensations, and in spite of a strong resistance he suddenly parted with his last meal into the lamps. The misfortune gave the captain more concern than the cabin-boy, who was in the condition that makes one feel that all earthly joys have passed away from you for evermore, and drowning would be a happy relief from the agony of it. Needless to say, he was soundly trounced for the misadventure; handy odds and ends were thrown at him; he was reminded of his daring promises on the eve of engagement, and an impassioned oration was delivered on the curse of engaging "useless rubbish who could not guide their stomachs when they got to sea." His troubles had begun. The flow of curses, which he now heard for the first time in his life, cut deeply into his little soul, and made him long to be landed, so that he might even wash doorsteps for a living rather than be subjected to such coarse abuse. Ah, but there was worse to come. This was merely a rude awakening. Could he have seen into the series of hardships and cruelties that lay in front of him, he might have deemed it better to close his desolating troubles by allowing the waves which swept over the vessel (as she was scudded along by the screaming wind) to bear him overboard into the dark.

Home-sickness or sentimental sensations were soon made to disappear by the busy life and rough, barbaric discipline enforced. First-voyage impressions live long in the memory. If they were not thrashed into permanent recollection, they were bullied or tortured into it by revolting methods of wrong which were recognised at that time in England to be legal. To their shame be it said, but how often have I heard men who had sprung from the masses and abject poverty, and who had succeeded in getting into position (so far as money would allow them to do so), deplore the introduction of a larger educational system and the enactment of more rigid laws to provide against a despotism that had become a national disgrace! And it was not until a few demoniacs had committed hideous murder, and were hung for it, that the legislature took the trouble to inquire into what was going on upon the high seas—nay, at times even before their very eyes.

One duty of a young sailor is to tar down the fore and aft stays. At any time and under any circumstances this was a precarious undertaking, and yet these fine young athletes would undertake it quite joyously, provided it was called for in the ordinary course of their duty, and there was no intimation or suspicion of it being intended as a "work-up" job, as they called it. The main and mizen stays stretched from mast to mast; the fore stays were more perpendicular, as they stretched from the masts to the jib-boom and bowsprit. It was usual to have a boatswain's chair to sit and be lowered down in while tarring these stays. Some mates disdained pampering youths with a luxury of this kind, so disallowed it, and caused them to sit in a bowlin' bight instead. But the most villainous thing of all was when a boy for a mere technical offence, perhaps, indeed, no offence at all, would be ordered to ride a stay down without either chair or bowlin'. The tar-pot was held in one hand, the tarring was done with the other, and the holding on was managed by a process of clinging with the legs and body as they slid along in a marvellously skilful way; and woe to the unhappy culprit who allowed any drops of tar to fall on the decks or paint-work! Sometimes these lads lost their balance and fell with their bodies under the stay, and failed to right themselves; in that case they had to slide down to where the stay was set up, get on top of it again, and climb up to where they had left off tarring. They were not allowed, even if they could have done so, to ride over the painted portion by sliding over it. Occasionally there occurred fatal falls, but this was a rare thing. I remember losing my balance while riding down a main top-gallant stay. The tar-pot fell to the deck, and I very nearly accompanied it.

There was much commotion caused by this mishap, as part of the contents of the bucket had splashed on the covering board and white-painted bulwarks. The exhibition of grief was far-reaching. The captain and his devoted officers made a great noise at me; they asked with passionate emotion why I didn't let my body fall instead—"there would have been less mischief done," said they! Of course they did not mean that exactly, though to the uninitiated it would have seemed uncommonly like it. The indications of combined grief and fearful swearing might have meant anything of a violent nature. I could not be disrated, as I was only a cabin-boy, but a substitutionary penalty was invoked against me. The chief officer, who had a voice and an eye that indicated whiskey, was a real artist in profane language. He vowed that as sure as "Hell was in Moses" I would never become worthy the name of a British sailor. This outburst of alcoholic eloquence touched me keenly, and ever since that time I have wondered wherein this original gentleman saw connection between the great Hebrew law-giver and the nether regions.

The cabin-boy's duties were not only numerous, but arduous. Under serious physical penalties he had to keep the cabin, its lamps and brass-work clean, and wash the towels and table-cloths. (The latter were usually made of canvas.) The skipper's and mate's beds had to be made, and washing done for them; small stores such as coffee, tea, sugar, biscuits, &c., were under the combined care of him and the commander. In addition to this, he had to keep all the deck brass-work shining; keep his watch and look-out; and, when he had learned how to steer, take his trick at the helm. If any of the small sails, such as royals, top-gallant sails, main top-gallant stay-sail, or flying jib had to be taken in, he was expected to be the first to spring into the rigging or along the jib-boom to do it, provided it was his watch on deck. It was really a sensational sight to witness these mannikins spinning up aloft and handling the flapping sail. I wonder now that more of them did not come to grief because of the stupid aversion many of the skippers had to allowing them to pass through what is known as the lubber hole—that is, a hole in the main-and fore-tops leading to the top-mast rigging. Occasionally both men and boys would lose their hold and fall on the rail, and be smashed to pieces. Sometimes they struck the rail, were killed outright, and then fell into the sea. And this is not to be wondered at when it is considered that their bodies were at right angles to the mast while passing over the round top from the main to the top-mast rigging. The mortality from this cause was, however, very small; such accidents generally occurred on cold, icy days or nights, when the hands had become benumbed. Yet it was amazing how these mere children managed to hold on at any time. But that is not all. If the vessel had to be tacked, it was the cabin-boy's duty to let go the square mainsail sheet when "tacks and sheets" was called; and when the order was given to "mainsail haul," that is, swing the main yard round, he had to haul in the opposite main sheet; and if he did not get it in so that the foot of the mainsail came tight up against the foremain shroud before the sail filled, he got into grievous trouble. If the vessel was at anchor in a roadstead, he had to keep his two-hour anchor watch the same as the rest of the crew. In beating up narrow channels such as the Swin, he was put in the main-chains to heave the lead and sing the soundings, and the sweet child-voiced refrain mingled with the icy gusts, which oft-times roared through the rigging whilst the cold spray smote and froze on him. Never a kind word of encouragement was allowed to cheer the brave little fellow, and his days and nights were passed in isolation until he was old enough and courageous enough to assert himself. The only peace that ever solaced him was when his watch below came, and he laid his poor weary head and body in the hammock. If the vessel was in port, and the shore easy of access, it was he who had to scull the captain ashore, and wait for him in the cold, still, small hours in the morning, until the pleasures of

grog and the relating of personal experiences had been exhausted. If the boy were asleep when the skipper came down, he got a knock on the head, and was entertained to a selection of oaths which poured forth until he got alongside the vessel. He was then told with strong manifestations of dignity to pass the painter aft; this done, he was rope-ended for having slept.

If the vessel were anchored in a road-stead, and the captain had to be rowed ashore, he had to be one of the crew of four, he pulling the bow oar, and, as soon as the rest landed, he was left in charge of the boat. The sequel to an incident of this kind is one of the most gruesome in the annals of maritime life. The captain of a vessel, anchored in Elsinore Roads, was rowed into the harbour. The crew of the boat were told that he would require them at 10.30 that night. The cabin-boy was left in charge, and the two A.B.'s and the oldest apprentice proceeded to a grog-shop, where they became more or less intoxicated. The captain had ordered a keg of gin to the boat, and at midnight he ordered the men to go off to the vessel with it, and come for him in the morning. They did not wish to go, as there was a strong south wind and current in the sound, but the captain insisted, and they went, with the result that the boat was picked up the following day covered with ice, and four dead bodies were the ghastly occupants of it.

Well nigh two years had passed away since our young friend planted his feet for the first time aboard ship. He had sailed far and learned much. The treatment he had been accustomed to made strong impressions on him; and he determined to emancipate himself from such tyranny the first opportunity he had; so that, when his vessel glided into a lovely landlocked harbour on the north-west coast of Ireland one bleak winter morning, his plan of escape having been secretly formed and kept, he determined to put it into force as soon as it was discreet to do so.

All hands having been paid off, excepting the mate and three apprentices, the task of cooking fell upon the cabin-

boy. He always had to do this when in a home port; that was another of his many functions, and not the least of them, which caused him very frequently to come to grief, though this young man had been impressed with the importance of learning to cook, amongst other things, long before he left home, so that, as a rule, he got along fairly well whenever it became his duty to work up a plain meal, which usually consisted of soup and doboys, that is, small dumplings boiled in the soup with the beef. A double-decker sea-pie was not only a favourite mess, but was considered even a luxury at that time, and most sailor-boys could cook it. It was made in a large pan or in the galley coppers, and consisted of the following ingredients: A layer of potatoes, small pieces of beef and onions well seasoned with pepper and salt, and covered over with water; then a deck of paste with a hole in the middle to allow the water to have free access, then more potatoes, beef, onions, and kidney, and then the final deck of paste, and a suitable amount of water were added. It was quite a common thing whilst these exploits of cookery were going on, for the skinflint skipper to stand over the boy, and if he detected him taking too thick a skin from the potato, he was lucky if he got off with a severe reprimand. It was usually an open-handed blow, intended sternly to enforce economy. Well, the vessel had been in port four days, and many acquaintances had been made by the cabin-boy, who had given his confidences to a select few. He was invited to go to a wake one night by the son of a gentleman who kept a shoe shop. This was an uproarious evening, from which he gathered new experiences. As he was ashore at liberty he deemed it prudent to be punctual in going on board. On getting on deck the master, who was standing on the poop, called him to him, and desired to know where he had been, and why he was ashore so late. He replied that he was not late, but aboard at the time his liberty had expired, and that he had been at a wake. The poor man nearly expired on the spot! He gasped in a screeching sort of tone, "A wake?

You damned young hemp! And your father a Protestant! I'll learn you to go to a wake! I'll teach you to disgrace your family and myself! No more shore for you, sir!"

And for the purpose of emphasising his displeasure the inevitable rope's-end was freely used, to the accompaniment of language that did not bear the impress of a saintly condition of mind, though he obviously derived comfort from the thought that he was upholding the dignity and traditions of the true Protestant faith. As soon as his conscience was appeased, he asked the Almighty's forgiveness for having used profane language, and ordered the boy to go to bed! He went to bed, but not to sleep; the result of his musings on these everlasting bullyings and thrashings was that at two o'clock in the morning he had packed all his bits of belongings into a bag, and woke an apprentice with whom he was on very cordial terms, to say goodbye before embarking on a new and unknown career. He had resolved to run away and conceal himself until the vessel had sailed, and then ship aboard an American barque which was in port. The other boy pleaded for him not to risk it, but his mind was made up. He would stand the insufferable tyranny no longer, and he went. He had anticipated what was going to happen by previously informing a well-to-do tradesman of his troubles and intentions, and so excited the sympathy of his wife and daughter as well as his own that they assured him of their hospitality and aid in carrying out the scheme of desertion. They admitted him into their home as soon as he presented himself, and he was treated with true Hibernian hospitality. The chief mate of the American barque was courting the daughter, a handsome young woman, whom he ultimately married. She was very solicitous in the poor lad's behalf, and it was decided that he should have a berth on the mate's ship, and in the presence of the youth she easily extracted a pledge from her lover that he would have him kindly treated. He felt in all probability the acme of joy in serving this amiable female, but soon there

came one of those accidents that break the current of human affairs. The boy thought he was safe after dark in paying a visit to the vessel he had practically shipped to serve aboard of, and took every precaution to avoid attracting attention. He had nearly got alongside when a hand was laid on his shoulder, and a kindly voice proclaimed him a prisoner. He was at first startled, but soon recovered self-possession, and seeing the gentleman was in plain clothes he demanded his right to interfere.

"This is my right," said he, showing a piece of paper, "and I may as well tell you that I am a detective, and have shadowed the house you are living in for several days. You must come with me. Your vessel is on the point of sailing, and I have instructions to take you aboard."

The boy appealed to the officer not to take him, as he would only run away at the first port again. The officer protested that he must do his duty; but, as he desired to say goodbye to the kind people who had given him shelter, he would stretch his instructions by taking him to them. They were deeply moved at the sight of the little culprit, and bade him an affectionate adieu. He and his clothes were given up to the irate captain, who received him with cold acknowledgment, and he was soon sailing towards a port in Scotland. After a quick run the vessel was docked and moored ready to receive cargo. The captain had been sullenly reticent on the passage. He spoke occasionally of base ingratitude and the extinction of the race, and how the object of his displeasure would be remembered when he got him into deep water again, and that he would teach him a salutary lesson for having broken his indentures and seeking refuge under the roof of an Irish Jesuit! Apart from these incoherent mutterings nothing of serious moment transpired. By way of preliminary chastisement, the boy was ordered to scrape the main-royal and top-gallant mast down during his watch below in the daytime, and neither the masts, nor the yards attached to them, received any real ben-

efit by this blockheaded notion of punishment. It is said, indeed, that they suffered materially. The fact of deriving pleasure by inflicting a cruel act on a mere child is hideous to think of, but in those days these uncultured, half-savage creatures were allowed all the powers of a monarch, and disdained the commonest rights of humanity. The captain was said to have expressed a sense of pride in what he termed the smart capture of his erring apprentice, and some talk was heard of the contemplated exploits of drilling after sailing again. Poor man! He was never to have the opportunity of gratifying an ignoble desire, for the night after the vessel's arrival the youthful incorrigible disembarked with a vow that he would never return to her again; and he kept his word. Could those fields and lanes in Scotland speak out the thoughts and the sufferings of the days that were spent there, what an ineffable record of woe they would lay bare!

Tramping by night, and concealed part of the way by day, this child of respectable parents was driven by cruel wrong to abandon himself to the privations of hunger, the rigour of a biting climate, and to the chance of his strength giving way before he had reached the destination that was to open out newer and brighter opportunities to him. Four weeks after deserting his vessel he landed at a large seaport on the north-east coast of England, and then began a new era. For many years he led a chequered and eventful life, which, however, did not prevent him from rising quickly to the head of his profession. Before he was twenty-two years of age he was given the command of a handsome sailing vessel, and at twenty-six he commanded a steamer. He had not seen his old captain for many years, though he often desired to do so. One day he came across him in London, and addressed him with the same regard to quarter-deck etiquette as he was accustomed to observe when a boy under his command. The old man liked it, and he observed with a quiver in his speech, "I am glad to notice that you have not forgotten what I took so much pains to learn you." His pupil assured him that he had not forgotten anything he had been taught, and especially the duty he owed to his old commander. The veteran was touched with the display of loyalty and the mark of respect shown him. There seemed to be an accumulation of recollections passing through his mind as he hesitatingly said, "I used to knock you about a good deal, but it was all for your good, and to teach you proper discipline." He was assured that everything of an unpleasant character had been shut out of the mind, so they parted with feelings of mutual cordiality. Some years had elapsed, when the young commander landed in a port in Denmark. A gentleman whom he knew told him a sad story of an English captain who had just died in the hospital under distressing circumstances. His illness had been brought on by his own excesses, complications set in, and after a few days' illness, he passed, through the valley of the shadow of death into Eternity. His bodily sufferings had been great, and his lonely desolation caused him unspeakable anguish. Death relieved him of both, and he was put to rest in a plain deal coffin. The vessels in port hoisted their flags half-mast, and a few seamen followed his remains to the tomb. The following day his old apprentice, whom he had driven from his presence thirteen years before, had two weeping willows planted at each end of the grave to mark the spot where his erring master rests; and he has visited it many times since.

CHAPTER IV

THE SEAMAN'S SUPERSTITIONS

The seamen of the fifties and sixties were grievously superstitious. They viewed sailing on a Friday with undisguised displeasure; and attributed many of their disasters when on a voyage to this unholy act. I have known men leave their vessel rather than sail on a Friday. The owner of a vessel who did not regard this as a part of the orthodox faith was voted outside the pale of compassion. Then it was a great breach of nautical morals to whistle when the wind was howling, and singing in such circumstances was promptly prohibited. If

perchance bad weather was encountered immediately after leaving port, and it was continuous, the forecastle became the centre of righteous discussion and intrigue, in order that the reason for this might be arrived at, and due punishment inflicted on the culprit who was found to be the cause of all their sorrows. They would look upon gales and mishaps, no matter how unimportant, as tokens of Divine wrath sent as a punishment for the sin of some one of them not having, for example, paid a debt of honour before sailing. The guilty person or persons were soon identified, even if they attempted to join in the secret investigation, and the penalty of being ostracised was rigidly enforced. It was a hard fate, which sometimes continued the whole voyage, especially if no redeeming features presented themselves. The sailor's calling makes superstition a part of his nature. The weird moaning of the wind suggests to him at times saintly messages from afar; and he is easily lost in reverie. He holds sweet converse with souls that have long since passed into another sphere, but the hallucinary charm causes him to fix his faith in the belief that they are hovering about him, so that he may convey to them some message to transmit to those friends or relatives who are the objects of his devout veneration. Yet he ceases to be a sentimentalist when duty calls him to face the realities of life. An order to shorten sail transforms him at once into another being. He usually swears with refined eloquence on unexpected occasions, when a sudden order draws him from visionary meditation. Dreams, which may be the creation of indigestible junk—that is, salt beef which may have been round the Horn a few times—are realities: privileged communications from a mystic source. There is great vying with each other in the relation of some grotesque nightmare fancy, which may have lasted the twentieth part of a second, but which takes perhaps a quarter of an hour to repeat; traverses vast space in a progression of hideous tragedy and calamitous shipwreck; and is served up with increased profusion of detail when the history of

the passage is manuscripted to their homes and to their lovers. Here is an instance of this mania in an unusually exaggerated form. For obvious reasons it is undesirable that the name of the vessel, or the captain, should be mentioned here. The captain had a dream, or, as he stated, a vision, when off Cape Horn bound to Valparaiso in a barque belonging to a South Wales port. The vessel had been tossed about for days with nothing set but close reefed topsails, amid the angry storming and churning of liquid mountains. One midnight, when eight bells had been struck to call the middle watch, there suddenly appeared on the poop the commander, who was known to be a man of God. He gave the order to hard up the helm and make sail. When she came before the wind the crew were puzzled to know the cause of this strange proceeding, and their captain did not keep them long in doubt. He called all hands aft, and when they had mustered he began: "Men, you know I believe in God and His Christ. The latter has appeared to me in a vision, and told me that I must sail right back to where we came from; and if I hesitate or refuse to obey the command the ship and all the crew will perish. " The crew were awestruck; the captain's statement gave rise to vivid stories of presentiments; while the luckless craft scampered back to the port where the unsuspecting owner dwelt. In due course the vessel arrived in the roads. A tug came alongside, and the captain was greeted in the orthodox nautical style. The supernatural tale was unfolded and the tug proceeded to convey the news of the arrival of the *T*——. The owner would have fallen on the neck of his captain had he been near. He wept with uncontrollable joy. His feelings swept him into ecstasies of generosity. Gifts of an unusual character for captains to receive were to be conferred upon him, and the owner longed for the flow of the tide so that his sentiments towards him might be conveyed in person. "Ah," said he, "how often have I said that Captain M—— was the smartest man that ever sailed from a British port! Just fancy, to make the voyage out and home in two and a half months! It is phenomenal!"

The master of the tug gaped at this local magnate in wonder, and thought that sudden lunacy had seized him. He blurted out, "Surely, Mr. J——, you have not lost your reason over this terrible misfortune?"

TELLING HIS FORTUNE

"Terrible misfortune?" repeated the impassioned owner. "Is it a terrible misfortune to make a West Coast voyage within three months?"

"No," said the burly tug master, "I now see you do not apprehend the position. I didn't care to say to you that the captain had a vision off Cape Horn which decided him to return to this port."

"What?" said the almost speechless potentate. "A vision? Back here, without being to Valparaiso? My God!—I will never get over it!"

And in truth he nearly collapsed, business, body, and soul, over the matter.

The vessel was brought into the harbour. The sanctified skipper did not receive the promised gifts! The vessel sailed in a few days without him for the same destination; and until a few years since he could be seen any day walking the quay, still holding to the belief that it was the Divine will he had carried out. This faith was strengthened by the vessel never having been heard of again

after sailing the second time. I never heard of the owner showing any vindictiveness to the poor captain, who was, no doubt, the victim of a strange hallucination.

It would be unfair to impute a monopoly of superstition to the seafarer. Sailors have superstitions which are not now exclusively theirs, though they may have been the originators of them; for instance, placing a loaf of bread upside down, spilling the salt (and nullifying the mischief by throwing a few grains over the left shoulder); these, as well as the leaving of stray leaves and stalks in teacups are considered sure indications of past or coming events, even by the large and enlightened public who pass their lives on dry land. There are few things more comical than to see the nautical person studiously avoid passing under a shore ladder. The penalty of it has a terror for him; and yet his whole life is spent in passing to and fro under rope ladders aboard ship without any suspicion of evil consequences. But the landsman's belief in mystic tokens and flighty safeguards is faint indeed compared with that which permeates and saturates the mind of the typical sailor. A gentleman with whom I was long and closely associated held definite opinions on symbolic apparitions. His faith in black cats was immovable; but this only extended to those who actually crossed his path, and to him that was a sign indicative of good fortune. I have seen him go into ecstasies of joy over an incident of this kind; and woe unto the person who interrupted the current of his happiness. He would curse him with amazing fluency until resentment choked the power of expression. This same human phenomenon was, in early life, shipwrecked on one of the hidden shoals with which the north-east coast abounds, at the very moment when he was taking from the girdle in the galley a hot cake he had baked in celebration of his birthday, and as a precaution against future calamities he ever after wore the left foot stocking outside in; and although he has passed through many dangers which nearly ended in

disaster, he has never again been shipwrecked. Hence his faith is unbroken in the protecting virtue of this mode of wearing that article of dress, and so is his reverent belief in black cats as charms against evil fortune. I have never known a person with a larger sense of genuine humour than this man possessed, and yet one could never appear to slight *his* peculiar superstitions without producing a paroxysm of fury in him. He would watch for the appearance of a new moon with touching anxiety, and although his finances were very frequently in a precarious condition, he never allowed himself to be without the proverbial penny to turn over under the new moon as a panacea against hidden pecuniary ills! If, in sailor parlance, a star "dogged the moon," that was to him a disturbing omen, and great caution had to be observed that no violation of nautical ethics took place during the transit. It was never regarded as a transit, but as a "sign" from which evil *might* be evolved.

Amidst all this singular piety in externals (for it was really a species of piety), this typical sailor never gave up his belief in the efficacy of strong language, which, among the worst of his class, was frequently indescribable; and the more eloquent he was in the utterance of oaths the larger became his conviction that he possessed a gift not to be acquired by mere tuition. Many years ago, when I was a very small apprentice boy aboard a brig we had a steward who was also a sailor of no common ability. His career had been a long one of varied villainy, he impersonating alternately a parson and a rich shipowner. In the latter *rôle* he succeeded in getting large advances of money from unsuspecting store, sail, and rope dealers—taking advantage of a trade-custom which prevails in every port, in return for which he gave orders, which caused the favoured firms to be looked upon with envy. They were requested to have these supplies put aboard four days after the order was given; and the penalty for not being able to do so was to be the loss of a very valuable connection. There was much condescension on the part of the bounteous customer, who "would call again in two days," and much thanking and bowing and shaking of hands on the part of the recipients when the time came to say "Good-day." The stores were duly sent to the docks where the vessels were lying, but the real owners did not recognise the person who had given the order as having any connection with them, whereupon an unhappy dawn broke over the minds of the unsuspecting victims. Many months elapsed before the gentleman in question was apprehended and confronted by the tradesmen to whom he owed a period of blissful dissipation. Needless to say the meeting was not so cordial as the parting, though a lack of cordiality could not be charged against the improvised shipowner. Indeed, to the great discomfort of his former friends, as soon as an opportunity was given him, from his position in the prisoners' dock, he saluted them with playful familiarity; but this did not prevent him being sent to penal servitude. He had played many other *rôles* under many names, but it was as a parson he prided himself in having met with success by the startling number of conversions that attended his efforts. He belonged to a respectable and well-known family, and their anxiety to have him reclaimed from the vices that had produced for them so much sorrow induced them to prevail on his brother-in-law, who was master of a brig, to take him under his special care; so he was appointed as steward, and thereby given the opportunity of spoiling much valuable food, and causing grievous dissension among the crew.

This loathsome creature could only be appealed to through his superstitions, and even the young apprentice boys soon discovered his weakness, and terrorised him whenever they got the chance. One awful morning in November, 1864, the vessel was hove-to under close-reefed main topsail. All hands had been on deck during the whole night, which was one of raging storm and disaster. The decks had been swept, and the galley carried away in the general destruction, so that no food could be cooked on deck. The captain gave orders to the steward to light a fire in the cabin stove, and make coffee for all hands. He proceeded to do this. The matches, however, had suffered in the commotion of the night, and would not ignite. After many futile efforts the steward's patience gave way; but certain members of the crew had impressed him with the conviction that the hurricane that was being encountered and the disasters that had befallen us were sent as a judgment on *him* for the blasphemous language he was accustomed to use at all times, whenever the slightest thing crossed his devilish nature. He put his hands on the table, his eyes were upturned, and with a softness of speech he slowly uttered, "Jesus wept—and so He might!" Of course he would have preferred a string of oaths as a relief to his pent-up anger. On the following night the hurricane still raged, and it was thought that something was wrong with the maintop-gallant sail. It looked as though it were blowing adrift. A hand was sent aloft to secure it, but when half-way up the top-mast rigging, he got on to the top-mast back stay, and slid down on deck. He was speechless for some time after reaching the deck. At last he jerkingly articulated that there was nothing wrong with the sail, but that which was believed to be sail was really some ferocious living thing. Whereupon great consternation spread; and volunteers were asked for to go aloft, and ascertain precisely what it was. It turned out to be an eagle, and after considerable difficulty a rope was got round it, and it was safely landed on deck. It so happened that shortly after the capture was made a tremendous sea struck the vessel, causing her to leak badly, and taking the remaining two boats overboard. This was put down not merely as a coincidence, but a coincidence that was sent for a purpose, and every mind was fixed upon the steward. The wretched man was stricken with panic. His thoughts centred on his past, and he became an abject drivelling confessionist, emptying himself of deeds that were awful to listen to, and had been kept to himself for years. The voyage soon ended, and the last I heard of him was that he was drinking himself to death; he had never got over the conviction that the Divine wrath was upon him.

The sight of a shark is an everyday occurrence in some latitudes. Nothing is thought of it, and sometimes much sport is derived in attempting a capture. But should a vessel be dogged for a succession of days by a shark, or (as very frequently happens) by a shoal of them, gloom begins to spread, imaginations begin to widen; whisperings and close consultations for evil purposes take place; and soon there has developed an epidemic of melancholia. Conjecture is rife. The explanation of it all is that these sharks have designs on human flesh, or they would not follow with such tenacity. There is much speculation as to how the unfortunate men are to be delivered into the grip of their ferocity, and whether the feast will involve the sacrifice of one or all of them. The more dismal the weather, the more impressive the danger becomes. Perchance a man falls overboard, or an accident occurs, no matter which; it is at once attributed to the proximity of the sharks. "They would never follow a vessel if they did not know they were to be rewarded by some tasty recompense." Indeed they were believed to have supernatural instincts as well as gluttonous intentions, which filled the sailor with alarm, and caused him to ponder uneasily over the idea of his last moments. It did not occur to him that these "slim" followers kept in close proximity to their vessel so that they might partake of the food that was daily cast into the sea; they are not particular whether it is human or not. What they look for is food. But Jack loves tragedy. He likes to imagine he is in danger of being eaten or robbed or imposed upon. The nonfulfilment of his prognostications does not humiliate him: it seems to inspire more tenacious belief.

The sea serpent, whatever that might be, has caused mariners of every age much perturbation. Periodically there are sensational reports emanating from some sea captain, that the real bleary-eyed monster has at last been discovered. Illimitable dimensions are given, together with much detail of its many peculiarities. Three years ago, in the month of May, I was cruising with some friends in my schooner yacht. We had traversed many of the Scottish Lochs, amongst them Loch Fyne, where the finest herring in the world abound, and are much sought after by fishermen as well as by bottle-nosed whales. We were making our way from Inverary towards Campbeltown, and as the wind was shy, off the north side of Arran, we were hugging the land in order to lead to our destination. A good wind was carried as far as Loch Ryan, when it slowly died away and became flat calm. One of my friends and myself were walking the deck together, when he excitedly observed, "What is that on our starboard beam; is it a reef?" I assured him there were no shoals in the vicinity of the yacht; and I took up the field-glasses, and saw quite plainly that it was a bottle-nosed whale. It soon began to move and send masses of water into the air. The calm continued, and some anxiety was felt lest the leviathan should playfully come towards us and test its power of lifting. It passed close to where we lay, and then shaped a course towards the opposite shore. Naturally our interest was excited, and as a favourable breeze sprang up and gradually strengthened we were able to follow at a discreet distance from the tail of the sea disturber. It would have taken the vessel out of our way to have followed it far, so a course was set for Campbeltown, and the monster was soon lost to view. Navigation was made intricate by a large fleet of fishing boats beating up towards the playground of the fish they sought to catch. The day following our arrival at Campbeltown this fleet re-entered the port, their crews stricken with a conviction that they had encountered the much-spoken-of sea-monster. Their tales varied only in degree, but their convictions were similar, and as they unfolded with touching solemnity the story of peril, the little town became the centre of wild, fluttering pulses. It was a conflict between pride of race and

sanctified horror, for had not their townsmen looked into the very jaws of death? One imaginative gentleman made a statement that was creepy in his version of a gallant fight against the demoniac foe. The monster is said to have raised itself high out of the water, and opened its jaws, which exposed to view a vast space, and suggested that the intention was to receive, if not a few of the boats, certainly a multitude of the people who manned them. One craft came gliding along, and the skipper promptly picked up an oar, and put it into the "serpent's" mouth, whereupon the oar was as promptly snapped asunder; and the skilful mariner sailed his craft gallantly out of harm's way while the cause of all the commotion went prancing about the ocean in defiance of the vast flotilla which is said at the same time to have occupied its attention. It would be impossible to give more than a summary of all the things that were said to have been done during this trying episode; and all that need be said now is that the men were stricken with awe. They remained in port for several days in the belief that their enemy was still on the rampage outside. Their deliverance had been miraculous; and no doubt much thanksgiving, and much petitioning for divine interposition, so that this visitor from a sinister world might be spirited away to some other locality, held their attention during the days that were spent under cover of a safe harbour. There can be little doubt that the cause of the fishers' frenzy was the quiet, inoffensive bottle-nosed whale, leisurely prowling about the Sound in search of a living, and, in fact, none other than the one that my friend had supposed to be a reef. These creatures rarely run amuck until the harpoon is thrust into them. They usually roll about the sea in the most harmless way. No doubt the sight of a huge creature in localities unaccustomed to it creates an impression of dull alarm, and, strange though it be, some minds are so constituted that their superstitions and imaginations are always thirsting after association with the nether regions.

A common belief among seamen is

that if rats migrate from a vessel that vessel is doomed; and many hardships have been endured at times on account of this belief. I am inclined to favour the idea that these creatures are just as tenacious of life as human beings are; but to say they have keener intuitive capacity than we is arrant nonsense. It is true they do not like leaky ships any more than their crews do; and they leave them for the same particular reasons as would induce them to leave districts on shore. Scarcity of food or comfort, or danger of attack, create their itinerant moods. Of course if their pasture is good they are difficult to get rid of. They are prolific and cling to their young. That unquestionably is a reason for their willingness to be driven from a position where the food supply may be precarious. They have their channels of communication which are as difficult to cut off as to find out, so that when they do leave a vessel that is in port it is pretty certain they have heard of some more comfortable quarters and a better playground. This accounts for them clearing out of a ship just before she sails, thus throwing some poor superstitious creature into abject fear that their exodus is the forerunner of calamity. To carry the superstition out logically, instead of rats being exterminated throughout a place or a vessel, they should really be encouraged to remain and multiply. I saw an extract from an American paper some years ago, and it told a sensational tale of a steamer which had arrived at Baltimore from Cuba, laden with iron ore. During the passage the whole crew were attacked by swarms of rats, which had come aboard at the loading port. The crew, including the captain, his wife, and family, were driven to take refuge on deck. The rats became infuriated for want of food, and boldly clamoured for it, until it was decided to feed them discreetly from the ship's stores. Many of the crew were bitten. Under less startling circumstances it is quite a common occurrence for seamen to have their toenails eaten off while they are asleep. It rarely happens that the flesh is penetrated; and they nearly always go for the big toe. People who have not seen such things are sure to be sceptical about the truth of this statement. It can, however, be easily verified. On the Baltimore vessel's arrival in the stream, and after communications had been effected with the shore, it was found that men could not be induced to risk working in the holds until the rats were expelled. It was decisively arranged to have the vessel scuttled. This was done, and the situation became more perplexing than ever. As soon as the water began to flow into the vessel, the rats took to the rigging, and every available space of it became occupied. Never had such a sight been witnessed before. It was decided to shoot at them. The panic at once grew into pandemonium, both amongst the rats and the public. The fear of large numbers of the rats making their escape seized the imagination, and took some subduing. Methods were adopted, however, which soon put an end to mere contemplation, and the rats were speedily put out of harm's way. The story comes from America, and is an answer to those who cling to the silly notion that rats have the faculty of prevision and always leave a ship that is to be sunk or is sinking. *These* rats would not leave even after the vessel was sunk.

Many years ago, long before sailing vessels succumbed to steam, I was serving as cabin boy aboard a brig laden with salt, which had been taken on board at St. Ubes, Portugal. We were in the Bay of Biscay, and had encountered a succession of gales from the time of leaving St. Ubes. The vessel had a private leak, that is, a leak which was not occasioned by constructive weakness, but by some omission of caulking, bolting, trinnelling, &c. This alone only called for one pump to be set going every two hours, but the heavy buffeting made her strain and leak so badly that it ultimately necessitated the continuous use of both pumps. The sea was running cross and heavy, which caused the cargo to shift, and the water to come on the ceiling, that is, the inner planking of the hull. A portion of the crew that could be spared from the pumps was ordered to take some forecastle bulkhead planks down, and make their way in-

to the hold for the purpose of trimming the cargo over. The work was carried on vigorously, amid a continuous flow of adjectives. The captain and owner, both of whom were much-respected men, were consigned by the sailors many times to perdition and other more or less sulphurous places. Indeed, the father of evil was freely invoked against them; but as both captain and owner are very much alive at the present time, the former controlling a vast business in conjunction with his sons, and the captain for many years having been living a peaceful life far away from the desolate storming of angry waters, whatever may be in store for those two well-cursed gentlemen, external appearances up to date favour the assumption that Jack's invocation has been unheeded. There was much desultory talk during the spells of shovelling, and one of the sailors, who, by the way, had at one time commanded his father's Scotch clipper, remarked, as though he were soliloquising, "I don't care a Scotch damn so long as the rats stick to us." Whereupon there arose a discussion upon the protective influence of rats, and it was decided that no leaky vessel should go to sea without them. One of the men thought he heard water coming in at the bow, and, as that part of the hold was not occupied with cargo, he made his way towards it, and asked me to bring him a light. He inquired if I heard anything. I replied in the affirmative. The carpenter was brought down into the hold, and the ceiling cut away; it was found that the rats had gnawed a hole through the *outside* planking, until they tasted tar and salt water. The sea pressure afterwards forced the skin in, and there became a free inlet of water. The hole was not large, but it had been sufficient to keep one pump going every two hours. There was now no doubt that this was the private leak. There was great rejoicing at the discovery, and after a few appropriate words, not necessary to reproduce here, against a Providence that could allow the perpetrators of such infinite mischief to prowl about attempting to scuttle ships, it was generally concluded that the occasion being one

of peril, should be allowed to pass without any stronger demonstration of reproach—as it might excite retaliation.

CHAPTER V

THE SEAMAN'S RELIGION

Nothing is more comic than the sailor's aversion to the person nautically recognised as the "sky-pilot." I have known men risk imprisonment for desertion, on hearing that a parson was going the voyage, or that the vessel was to sail on a Friday. If any of them were asked their reason for holding such opinions, they would no doubt make a long, rambling statement of accidents that had happened, and the wild wrath that follows in the wake of a ship sailing on the forbidden day! These prejudices still survive in a modified form. The younger generation of seamen do not view the presence of the parson on board their ship with any strong objection. In many cases he is rather welcomed than otherwise. But the last generation had a strong tradition, which could not be subdued, that no clerical gentleman should be looked upon with favour as a passenger. The boycott was sometimes carried out against him during the voyage with unrelenting cruelty. Ever since the Lord commanded Jonah, the son of Amittai, to arise and go to Nineveh, and the Hebrew preacher took passage aboard the ship of Tarshish instead, there has been trouble. The senseless antipathy has been handed down the ages, and the legacy comes from a shameless gang who were cowardly assassins, from the skipper downward! Poor Jonah! The tempest did not unnerve *him*; for, while the other drivelling creatures were chucking their wares overboard, he slept peacefully, until the bully of the crowd, and no doubt the greatest funk, called out to him, "What meanest thou, O sleeper? Arise, call upon thy God, if so be that God will think upon *us* that we perish not!" These creatures always want sacrifices made to save their own precious skins; and they found in the poor penitent Hebrew a willing sacrifice. He *agreed* that they should cast him into the sea! It is not recorded what methods of torture were used in order to extract his consent; but it is pretty safe to assume that the Tarshish crew made it so hot for the poor man that he was glad to say to them, "Take me up and cast me forth into the sea!" Thus it comes to pass that the race of seamen cling to a tradition which originated in craven ignorance.

Some years ago a large party was invited by me to a trial trip of a new steamer. Amongst the guests were a number of ministers, some of whom were my personal friends, and some the friends of others who had been invited. A gentleman who had been in my service for many years held strongly to the old tradition against clerics, and vowed that no good would ever come of such a reckless breach of nautical etiquette. He felt assured that much ill would come of it. His countenance the whole day betokened internal conflict! He refused to be ridiculed into consolation, and I think has felt chagrined ever since that nothing has happened to justify his prophecy. It must not be supposed, however, that men holding these views carried their resentment ashore. Many of them were on easy terms of friendship with sky-pilots, and listened to their devotional efforts and teaching with fervent submission. A story, which is known and reverently believed by the typical sailor, has done service many times. It is this: A parson had embarked aboard a sailing vessel as a passenger. They were crossing the Bay of Biscay when a tempest began to rage and the darkness became full of trouble. The sea lashed with remorseless effect on the hull of the vessel, until her timbers cracked and made strange noises. It was discovered that the vessel was leaking badly, and all hands were ordered to the pumps. The hurricane continued to roar, and the parson became alarmed at the tumult. He at last appealed to the captain to know whether the danger was of a serious character. The captain informed him the danger was great; but, if he desired to be *assured* of his safety or otherwise, he was to go towards the men that were pumping and listen whether they were swearing. If they were, there

was no immediate danger. He came back and said to the captain, "Glory be to God, they are swearing!" A short time was allowed to elapse, and another visit was paid. He came back and informed the commander that they were still swearing, but not quite so hard; "Indeed," said he, "I thought I heard some of them praying." "Ah," said the captain, "I fear if hard swearing does not continue, and they begin to pray, there will be no hope!" Whereupon the man of Holy Orders dropped on his knees and offered up an eloquent supplication for Divine aid: "O God, in Thy boundless compassion do Thou cause these sailors to cease praying, and make them to swear with a vigour and force that will appease the anger of the waves, and bring Thy servants out of danger into safety!" The captain called out "Amen," and added a supplementary petition for their deliverance, which is said to have been granted.

Sailors of that day spoke of God with the profound belief that He was their exalted fellow-countryman, and they did not scruple to charge Him with indifference to their nautical interests, if a foreigner, or a foreign vessel, happened to gain a monetary or seafaring advantage over them. This is not a mere legend. North Blyth, in the county of Northumberland, was inhabited by personalities who held definite opinions on these matters. One old gentleman, whom I remember very well (his name was Readford, but he had the distinction of being better known as "Barley"—why he was given this name there is no need to relate), held very strong views as to the functions and obligations of the Almighty. He never doubted His existence or His power, and he always claimed a dispensation of benefit as the right of British patriots.

The following story, true in every essential, will show his reasons for doing so: Barley was in command of a collier, which traded between Blyth and London. On one of his voyages to London he encountered a strong head-wind, which caused him to have to beat "up Swin." A Dutch galliot—type of vessel which has never had the reputation of

being a racer—was in company, to leeward of him. Barley managed by dexterous manipulation to keep her there until the flood tide was well-nigh spent; but, alas for human fallibility, and the eccentric fluctuations of the wind, the Dutchman stood towards the north shore, while our hero, who was priding himself on the superior qualities of himself and his brig, stood towards the south, whereupon the Dutchman got a "slant of wind" which came off the north shore. The result was the British vessel was badly weathered by the galliot. Barley's anger could not be appeased. It was an offence against national pride and justice! He forthwith called the attention of his chief officer to the indignity that had been thrust upon them. "Look," said he, in wrathful humiliation, "there's God Almighty given that adjective Dutchman a leading wind and allowed His own countryman to be jammed on a lee shore!" It was said that Barley never really forgave this unpatriotic act, though he still adhered to the belief that the God of British seamen was stedfastly on the side of conservatives of every kind!

There is no class of workmen that is so much thought of and cared for as the sailor class, and there is none who need and deserve such consideration more. It would be invidious to draw comparisons between classes, so that all I have to say on the point is that they have always compared favourably with those whose avocation is different from theirs. They are susceptible to good or evil influences. Perhaps not more susceptible to one than to the other; and considering the malevolent, thievish scoundrels by whom they are continually beset, their record does not compare badly with that of others. Vagrancy is almost unknown amongst them, and if their vices are large their temptations are great; but, take them as a whole, they seldom premeditate evil. Their intentions are mostly on the side of right and goodness. Some of them stand like a rock against being tempted by the gangs of harpies that are always hovering about them. Others allow their good intentions to vanish as soon as the predatory gentlemen with their seductive methods make their appearance. Agencies such as the Church of England Missions to Seamen and the Wesleyan Methodist Mission are to be thanked for the hard efforts made to keep the sailor out of harm, and to reclaim those who have fallen. They may be thanked also for having been the means of diminishing, if not altogether extirpating, a loathsome tribe of ruffians who were accustomed to feast on their blood. These Missions are a Godsend not only to the sailor, but to the nation. No other agency has done the work they are doing. The Church is apt, to gather its robes round a cantish respectability, and call out "Save the people," and the flutter falls flat on the seats. These missions owe any success they have had to going *to* the people.

A few wholesome women are worth scores of men in getting at sailors—or for that matter in getting at anybody else, and the importance of getting more of them attached to the work should not be overlooked. The sailor is a person of moods. Sometimes it is religion, and sometimes it is something very different, and it is only those women who have grace, comely looks and supreme tact, and who carry with them a halo of bright cheerfulness, who can deal successfully with cases of this kind. The long-faced, too much sanctified female, doling out fixed quantities of monotonous nothings, is an abomination, and is calculated to drive man into chronic debauchery. One look from this kind of awful female is a deadly agony, and much effort should be used to avoid her. But there are even men engaged in religious work, whose agonising look would give any person of refined senses the "jumps." What earthly use are such creatures to men who crave for brightness and hope to be put into their lives, and the passion of love to be beamed into their souls? If people would only bear in mind that it is always difficult to find a real soul behind a flinty face, a vast amount of mischief would be obviated by making more suitable selections for philanthropic and religious work. Of course there is more needed than a

pleasant look. It is imperative that there should be combined with it knowledge, and the knack of communicating it. All denominations have wasters thrust upon them, sometimes by the ambition of parents that their sons should be ministers, and sometimes by the unbounded belief of the young men themselves in their fitness. But it often becomes apparent that good bricklayers or blacksmiths have been spoiled in the process of selection; whereas a little courage and frankness on the part of the selection people would have saved many souls and many reputations.

CHAPTER VI

SAFETY AND COMFORT AT SEA

The present-day sailor has a princely life compared with that of his predecessors of the beginning and middle of the last century. Those men were ill-paid, ill-fed, and for the most part brutally treated. The whole system of dealing with seamen was a villainous wrong, which stamps the period with a dirty blot, at which the British people should be ashamed to look. What awful crimes were permitted by the old legislatures of agricultural plutocrats! Ships were allowed to be sent to sea in an unseaworthy condition. Men were forced to go in them for a living, and scores of these well-insured coffins were never seen or heard of again after leaving port. Their crews, composed sometimes of the cream of manhood, were the victims of a murderous indifference that consigned them to a watery grave; and the families who survived the wholesale assassination were left as legacies of shame to the British people, who by their callousness made such things possible. Whole families were cast on the charity of a merciless world, to starve or survive according to their fitness. Political exigencies had not then arisen. The people were content to live under the rule of a despotic aristocracy, and so a devastating game of shipowning was carried on with yearly recurring but unnoticed slaughter. In one bad night the billows would roll over hundreds of human souls, and no more would be heard of them, except, perhaps, in a short para-

graph making the simple announcement that it was feared certain vessels and their crews had succumbed to the storms of such and such dates. "Subscription lists for sailors' wives, mothers, and orphans! Good heavens! What is it coming to? *They* have no votes! What, then, do they want with subscriptions?" "But you subscribe for colliery, factory, railroad, and other shore accidents. What difference does it make how the bereavement occurs?" "Votes make the difference—the importance of that should not be overlooked!"

In disdain of the commonest rights of humanity this nefarious business was allowed to flourish triumphant. The bitter wail of widows and orphans was silenced by the clamour for gold until all nature revolted against it. The earth and the waters under the earth seemed to call aloud for the infamy to be stayed. The rumbling noise of a vigorous agitation permeated the air. Strenuous efforts were made to block its progress. Charges of an attempt to ruin the staple industry of the country were vociferously proclaimed and contemptuously unheeded. Parliament was made the centre of intrigue, whereby it was expected to thwart the plans of the reformers, and throw legislation back a decade, but the torrent rushed along, with a spirit that broke through every barrier. Even the great Jew, Benjamin Disraeli, funked further evasion and opposition, after the memorable evening when Samuel Plimsoll electrified the House, and stirred up the nation, by charging the Prime Minister with the responsibility of proroguing Parliament in order that shipping legislation should be evaded, and further charged him with indifference to the loss of life at sea! The onslaught was so fierce and irresistible that it became a necessity not only to listen but to act. Thus it came to pass that a hitherto obscure gentleman, who had no connection whatever with the sea, was the means of carrying into law one of the most beneficent pieces of legislation that has ever been introduced to the House of Commons; and his name will go down to distant ages, with renown unsurpassed in the pages of Mercantile

History. And shame to him who would detract from the great reformer his share in the act which has been the means of saving the lives of multitudes of seamen, and which has stamped upon it the immortal name of Samuel Plimsoll.

Drastic reforms cannot be brought about without causing inconvenience and even suffering to some one; and I am bound to say a vast amount of unnecessary hardship was caused in condemning unseaworthy vessels, many of which belonged to poor old captains who had saved a bit of money, and invested it in this way long before there was any hint of the coming legislation which was to interfere, and prevent them from being sailed unless large sums of money were expended on repairs. Scores of these poor fellows were ruined. Many of them died of a broken heart. Many became insane; not a few ended a miserable existence by taking their own lives; or died in almshouses, and under other dependent conditions. Of all classes of men, I do not know any who have such an abhorrence for the poorhouse as the sailor class. They will suffer the greatest privations in order to avoid it. It was a hard, cruel fate to have the earnings of a lifetime, and the means of livelihood, taken from them by a stroke of the pen, without compensation; and England again degraded herself by substituting one crime for another. These fine old fellows had been at one time a grand national asset; some of them had fought our battles at sea; but even apart from this some compensation should have been voted to all those who were to be affected by legislation that was sprung upon them, and passed into law for the public good. It may be said that any scheme of compensation must face heavy difficulties, but that is not a sufficient reason for not grappling with the question.

Compensation to the cattle-owners during the cattle plague was difficult no doubt to adjust. Indeed all revolutionary schemes are surrounded with complexities that have to be got over; but in the hands of skilled, willing workmen they can be carried out. Not very long ago a political party introduced a scheme for compensating the publicans—ostensibly because drunkenness would be diminished. It bubbled over with difficulties, but it would have been passed into law had the other party of the state not intervened in such a way as to prevent it. The same political party which thought it right that the publicans should be compensated, were not unmindful of some more of their friends, and voted something like five million sterling per annum to be distributed among landowners, parsons, &c. When the poor old sailors, withered and broken by hard usage, pleaded, for pity's sake, not to be ruined, their appeals were ruthlessly ignored.

A most extraordinary feature of the agitation to prevent loss of life at sea was the attitude of some shipmasters. They believed it to be an undue interference with their sacred rights. At the time when Mr. Plimsoll was vigorously pushing his investigations into the causes for so many vessels foundering, he went to Braila and Galatz, and examined every English steamer he was allowed to visit. Some owners, hearing that he was on a tour of investigation, instructed their captains not to allow him admittance; and I heard at the time that these instructions in some cases were rudely carried out. One forenoon he paid a casual visit to the steamer "*A——*," and entered into conversation with a person whom he assumed to be the commander. He chatted some time with him upon general topics, and soon discovered that the captain was not of the same political faith as himself. Shipmasters who take political sides are generally conservative. Up to that time he had carefully avoided making known his identity. At last he ventured to approach the object of his visit. He said, "Now, Captain, we have had a pleasant little chat; I should like to have your views before I go, on the Plimsoll agitation. They may be of value to me. I should like you to state also what you think of Plimsoll. I have heard varied opinions of him."

"Well," said the captain, in broad North Shields dialect, "you ask what I think of the agitation. My opinion is that all the skallywags who are taking part in it should be locked up, and have the cat every morning at five o'clock, and every hour of the day after, until they abstain from meddling with what they know nothing about! And as for Plimsoll, I would tie one end of a rope round his neck, and attach the other to a fire bar, and chuck him in there," pointing to the ebbing stream of the Danube!

"Then," said Mr. Plimsoll, "you are not in sympathy with the movement?"

"No," said the infuriated skipper, "and nobody but a —— fool would be!"

"But don't you think, Captain," said Mr. Plimsoll, "that the measures you suggest are somewhat extreme, for after all they are only trying to improve the condition of the seamen?"

"Seamen be d——d," said this meteoric Northumbrian. "We don't want ships turned into nurseries, and that's what it's coming to!"

There were indications that the interview should cease. Mr. Plimsoll thereupon prepared to take his leave. He apologised to the captain for having taken up so much of his time, handed him his card, and proceeded to land. The gallant captain looked at the card, and called for his distinguished visitor to wait, so that he might make known to him that he was ignorant of his identity, otherwise he would have saved him the pain of disclosing his opinions!

"And your method of putting a stop to agitation?" interjected Plimsoll.

"Well," said the rollicking mariner, laughing at the joke that had been played upon him, "we sailors express ourselves *that way*, but we have no bad intentions!"

"I apprehend that is the case, Captain," said Plimsoll.

So ended an interview which is memorable to at least one person; and not least notable for the friendship Mr. Plimsoll showed towards his would-be executioner! The story was told to me about two months after the interview occurred by the captain himself. It is very odd that even one man, especially a shipmaster, should have been found disagreeing with a reform that was to be of so much benefit to all classes of seafaring men.

Up to that time vessels were sent to sea scandalously overladen. There was no fixed loadline as there is now. Cargoes were badly stowed; no bagging was done. The fitting of shifting boards was left pretty much to the caprice of the master, who never at any time could be charged with overdoing it, but rather the reverse. I am speaking now more particularly of steamers, though to some extent the same reckless disregard for human safety existed among sailing vessels. It was necessary, however, that commanders of "windjammers" should be more painstaking in the matter of having their cargoes thoroughly stowed, and that adequate bulkheads and shifting boards should be fitted; for the shifting of a sailing vessel's cargo was accompanied with the possibilities of serious consequences. Sailing vessels cannot be brought head-on to wind and sea, as steamers can, and the weather may be so boisterous as to make it impossible to get into the holds; and even if these are 'accessible, the heavy "list" and continuous lurching prohibit the trimming of the cargo to windward.

But the great loss of life was not altogether caused by allowing rotten, leaky, badly equipped sailing vessels to go to sea, nor by the neglect of commanders of both sailers and steamers to adopt reasonable precautions for the purpose of avoiding casualty. At the very time when the whole country was ablaze with excitement over the harrowing disclosures that investigation had brought to light, Lloyds' Classification Committee was allowing a type of narrow-gutted, double-decked, long-legged, veritable coffins to be built, that were destined to take hundreds of poor fellows to their doom. Their peculiarity was to capsize, or continuously to float on their broadsides. Superhuman effort could not have kept them on their legs. Neither bagging transverse or thwartship bulkheads were of any avail. Scores of them that were never heard of after leaving port found a resting-place, with the whole of their crews, at the bottom of the Atlantic Ocean. They lie there, unless enormous pressure has crushed them into mud; and their tombs, could they be revealed, would give ghastly testimony to the incompetence of naval architects. No amount of precautionary measures could have made this type of craft seaworthy. They were not shaped to go to sea. My own impression is, apart from the crankiness of these rattletraps, there was a vast amount of overloading which was the cause of many vessels being sent to the bottom; so many, indeed, that it became a common saying among seamen who were employed in the Baltic trade that if the North Sea were to dry up it would resemble a green field, because of the quantity of green steamers that had perished there. Perhaps the phrase was merely a picturesque figure of speech, as the North Sea makes no distinction as to the claim it has on its victims, and the colour of paint does neither attract nor repel its favour. Notwithstanding the startling evidence which proved that there was something radically wrong in the design and construction of what was known as the "three-deck rule" type, Lloyds' Classification and the Board of Trade officials adhered to the idea of their superiority over every other class. The Hartlepool Well-decker became the object of hostility. It was pronounced by dignified theorists to be unsafe. The long wells combined with a low freeboard lacerated their imaginations. They could not speak of it without exhibiting strong emotion. "Suppose," said they, "a sea were to break into the fore well and fill it, the vessel would obviously become overburdened. Her buoyancy would be *nil*, and she would succumb to the elements."

But practical minds had provided against such an eventuality. These objects of aversion had what is called a raised quarter-deck; two ends which stood boldly out of the water, and of course a big "sheer." Heavy seas rarely came over their bows or sterns, and when they did the bulk of the water did not remain or seem to affect their buoyancy. The heaviest water was taken aboard amidship, when they were running with a beam sea or scudding before a gale; but owing to their great sheer it gravitated in a small space against the bridge bulkhead, the structure of which was strong enough to stand excessive pressure. They were considered to be the finest and safest tramps afloat by men who sailed in them. Vessels of two thousand tons deadweight, with only eighteen to twenty-four inches freeboard, would make winter Atlantic passages without losing a rope-yarn, while many of the three-deckers with six or seven feet freeboard never reached their destination. Still the theorists kept up their unreasoning opposition to the Well-deckers, and the Hartlepool men were driven to take the matter up vigorously. They would have no indefinite, haughty assertions. They demanded investigation; and the result of it proved that the theorists were wrong, and the men of practical ideas were right. It was proved that there were singularly few cases of foundering among these vessels, and that fewer lives were lost in them than in any others. This is not the only instance in which Lloyds' Classification Committee have been proved wrong in their opinions. They refused in the same way, for some time, to class Turrets. I was obliged to give up a conditional contract which I had made with Messrs. Doxford and Sons, of Sunderland, for the first built of these, in consequence of their refusal to class. But Turrets have now been well tested, and prove very superior sea-boats. Underwriters, indeed, could not have better risks; and, what is as good a test as any of a vessel's seagoing qualities, is the readiness of seamen to join and their reluctance to leave it.

But each successive depression in shipping unrolls the resources of the mind, and there are evolved new ideas which disclose advantages hitherto unknown. They may not be great, but they are usually sufficient to make it possible to carry on a profitable trade instead of stopping altogether or working at a loss. It was this that brought the Switchback into existence: a vessel, by the way, which has a short, deep well forward; a long bridge; raised after deck; and a long well and poop aft. Then came the Turret, and then the Trunk; and last, the

Single Decker on the "three-deck rule." I do not believe it possible that any of these will ever founder if they are properly handled, if their cargoes are properly stowed, and if no accident to machinery or stearing-gear occurs. They may come into collision with something, run on to a sand-bank or reef, and then founder, but not by force of hard buffeting. I am persuaded that the chances are a thousand to one in favour of them pulling through any storm in any ocean. But this is not all that can be said of them. The men that compose the crew have spacious, comfortable, healthy quarters, whereas in the old days, besides the prospect of being taken to Davy Jones's locker, men were housed in veritable piggeries: leaky, insanitary hovels, not good enough to bury a dead dog in.

CHAPTER VII

WAGES AND WIVES

When I first went to sea, and for many a long day after, I used to hear the sailors who were more than a generation my seniors, talking of the wages they received during the Russian war aboard collier brigs trading from the north-east coast ports to London, France, and Holland. They used to speak of it with restrained emotion, and pine for an outbreak of hostilities *anywhere*, so long as it would bring to them a period of renewed prosperity! Able seamen boasted of their wages exceeding by two or three pounds a voyage what the masters were getting. It was quite a common occurrence at that time for colliers to be manned entirely with masters and mates. They stowed away their dignity, and took advantage of the larger pay by accepting a subordinate position. Of course it was the scarcity of men that gave them the opportunity. They were paid in some cases nine to twelve pounds a voyage, which occupied on an average four weeks. The normal pay was four to five pounds a voyage for each man, all food, with the exception of coffee, tea, and sugar, being found. The close of the big war brought, as it always does, a reaction, and it is safe to say that collier seamen have never

been paid so liberally since. The racing with these extraordinary craft was as eagerly engaged in as it was with any of the tea clippers. It was an exciting feature of the trade which carried many of them to their doom almost joyously. Their masters were paid eight pounds per voyage, and if their vessels were diverted from coasting to foreign trades their stipend was eight to nine pounds a month. Considering the cost of living in those days, it is a marvel how they managed, but many of them did not only succeed in making ends meet, but were able to save. They owed much to the frugal habits of their bonny, healthy wives, who for the most part had been domestic servants, or daughters of respectable working men, living at home with their parents until they were married. They were trained in household economy, and they were exclusively domesticated. Educational matters did not come into the range of their sympathies. They were taught to work, and they and their homes were good to look upon. Many of these thrifty girls married swaggering young fellows who were before the mast. They were not merely thrifty, but ambitious. Their ambition was to become captains' wives; nor did they spare themselves to accomplish their desire promptly. They did not overlook the necessity of inspiring their husbands with high aims, and in order that their incomes might be improved these married men were coaxingly urged to seek an engagement as cook— a post which carried with it ten shillings per month more than the able seamen's pay, besides other emoluments, such as the dripping saved by skimming the coppers in which the beef or pork was boiled, and casking it ready for turning into cash wherever the voyage ended. The proceeds, together with any balance of wages, were handed over to the custody of the imperious lady, who was continuously reminding the object of her affection that he should apply himself more studiously to learning during his voyages, so that he would have less time to stay at the navigation school, and more quickly achieve nautical distinction when their savings amounted to

the sum required for passing the Board of Trade examination first, only mate, and then for master. But once they got their mate's certificates, financing became easier; and, although domestic expenditure might have increased, the good lady steadily kept in view the joy that would light up their home and come into her life when she could hear her husband addressed by the enchanting title of "Captain!" Hence the effort to save became a fixed habit.

When their object was attained, and the husband had passed his examination successfully, he soon got a command, and although the pay was small many of these men, with the assistance of their wives, saved sufficient to take an interest in a vessel. This was an achievement never to be forgotten. The news spread quickly over a large district. The gossips became greatly engaged, and the distinguished person was the object of respectful attention as he walked up and down the quays or public thoroughfares with an air of sanctified submission. It was a great thing to become part owner of a vessel in those days when large dividends were so easily made, and a small share very often led up to considerable fortune.

It is not to be supposed that the only road to success was through the galley doors. I do not mean that at all. There were scores of men that became shipmasters on our north-east coast who never sought the opportunity of figuring in the galley, and even if they had they could not have cooked a potato without spoiling it! It has long been a saying among sailors that "God sends grub and the devil sends cooks," and the saying is quite as true to-day as it was when cooks had not the advantages they have now of attending cookery classes. I merely relate the story of how a number of these men of the middle of last century added to their incomes in order that they might not stint their families of the necessaries of life, and at the same time might put aside a little each voyage until they had accumulated sufficient to enable them to stay ashore and pass the necessary examination. How a certain section of these men acquired their diplomas will always be a mystery to themselves and to those who knew of them. They were sailors every inch, and they claimed no higher distinction. It would be ridiculous to suppose that they were representative of the higher order of captain. With these they had nothing in common. Indeed, they were a distinct race, that disdained throwing off forecastle manners; whereas the higher type of captain, wherever he went, carried with him a bright, gentlemanly intelligence that commanded respect. The higher class of man nearly always soared high in search of a wife, not so much in point of fortune as in goodness, education, useful intellectual attainment—a lady in fact, combining domestic qualities compatible with his position. The merely intellectual person did not appeal to him. It was rational culture he sought for, a companionable woman indeed, who could use her hands as well as her head. Sometimes their judgment erred, and carried them into a vortex of misery.

The swift pulsations of a generous heart generally do lead to trouble if not well steadied by sound judgment. One of the most pathetic instances of this I have ever heard of occurred to a man who was high up in his profession. I knew him well. He was held in high esteem by his many friends. But his big soul was too much for him. He made the acquaintance of a young lady who intoxicated his fancy. She was beautiful: a quick, attractive girl of twenty-one, who could talk brightly of things that excited his attention. Soon she told him a piteous tale of domestic trouble. She was an artist in words and facial expression. Her whole being was indicative of a guileless life. One morning by appointment they met to say goodbye, for he was to sail from London that afternoon in command of a large vessel on a long voyage. She was brimming over with sparkling wit that overjoyed him. She skilfully hinted of marriage on his return, and playfully adjured that he should not allow other attractions when he was abroad to lessen his affection for her.

"Ah," said she, "sailors are so good, I fear you may not be an exception."

"Well," said he, "as you seem to have some doubt as to my *bonâ-fides* I think the question may be settled by my marrying you now."

"What!" said the fair maiden, "this forenoon? Surely you will allow me to consult my mother?"

"No," said the captain; "that would spoil the romance, and make it uninteresting. We must be spliced at once." And they were. The result was a ghastly tragedy. The lady turned out a termagant. Happily she did not live long, but while she lived it was terrible. He told me the tale long after, and the pathos of it, in all its hideous detail, was piteous. It sank deep into his life, and changed his whole character. He was a man of culture, and in the affairs of life displayed unusual common sense. No one could comprehend how he came to be drawn into this ill-assorted union, that might have sacrificed two lives.

There is no body of men who should be so careful in choosing their wives as sailors, no matter what their rank may be. If they have children, the sailor, or captain, sees little of them, and can have no part in their training, whereas the mother has it in her power to fashion their lives either for good or evil. She is always with them, and the responsibility of forming their characters must rest almost entirely with her. It would be a reckless exaggeration to say that all successful men had good wives; but I think it safe to assume that a large majority of them are blessed in that way. One thing is certain, if you see a well-conditioned, well-behaved child, there is a good mother and a good wife behind it. And it may not be unsafe to assert that the successful man nearly always owes some of his success to his wife's assistance. She may not have assisted actually in the business itself, but she may have done better still by holding her tongue at the proper time, and watching a suitable opportunity of making an appropriate suggestion, avoiding saying or doing anything that will irritate and break the continuity of thought which is essential to the husband's success. A great deal may be achieved by

discreet silence.

The wages of captains sailing in north-east coast brigs and barques that traded to the Mediterranean, Brazils, West Indies, and America, ranged from ten to twelve pounds per month. Those trading to the East Indies received fourteen pounds, and some out of their wages had to find charts and chronometers. London owners paid higher wages to their captains, but less in proportion to their crews. These commanders were on the whole a very intelligent, well-conducted lot of men. They had high notions, perhaps, of their importance, but they did no ill to anybody by this. There were occasional squabbles between their mates and themselves, and sometimes bickerings with the crew, but these were never of a very serious or lasting character; in fact, I have known men sail for years with one captain, and it was delightful to witness the treatment and mutual respect shown to each other. The men were frequently far more jealous of their captain's dignity than he was himself. There were others whose dignity became a slavish occupation to sustain. It sometimes happened if the master and mate differed on some minor matter that their relations became childishly strained, and each asserted his rights until the feeling softened. The captain always claimed the starboard side of the quarter-deck as his special parading ground, the mate the port. It often happened when these disagreements occurred the master, to show his authority more drastically, would ask the carpenter for a piece of chalk and draw a line down the centre of the deck. When this was done the aggrieved commander would address his chief officer in a deep, hollow voice that was obviously artificial. "Sir," or "Mr.," he would begin, "I wish to impart to you that your conduct has been such as to cause me to draw this line so that our intercourse may not be so close as it has been. Please do not presume to attempt any familiarity with me again; stick to your own side!" This piece of grotesque quarterdeck-ism was made all the more comical by the serious way it was taken by the mate and enforced by the master!

It did not occur to *them* that there was something extremely humorous in it. Another ludicrous custom was this: if the master and mate were on deck together, though there was ample room for both to walk on the weather side, the mate was always supposed to give way to the captain, and walk on the lee side, no matter what tack the vessel was on. If the officer in charge was smoking, and either standing or walking on the weather side, and the captain came on deck, immediately the short cutty pipe was taken out of his mouth, and, as a mark of respect, he passed to leeward! It was considered the height of ill-manners for a mate or second mate to smoke a churchwarden or a cigar!

The food that was supplied to these north country "southspainers" was neither plentiful nor good. It was not infrequently bought in the cheapest and nastiest markets—in fact, it is not an exaggeration to say that large quantities of it were not fit for human beings to eat.

The owners were, as a rule, of humble birth. Many of them inherited frugal habits from their parsimonious parents, and many of them became miserable misers independent of any hereditary tendency. If their generous impulses ever did swell big enough to give the captains a few delicacies, they were overcome with fear lest extravagance should enter into their lives, and therefore they hastened to caution them with imploring emphasis to take special care not to allow too much to be used, as luxuries of that kind were very costly! The captains were put to sore straits at times to carry out the wishes of their owners in doling out the food; and it often happened in the process of economising they became imbued with the same greedy ways as their employers. It would not be fair to charge all northeast coast owners of that period with the shame of stinting their crews of proper food; those who did so had no idea that they could be accused of being criminally mean. Their lean souls and contracted little minds could only grasp the idea of making money, and hoarding it after it was made. Hundreds of fine fellows had their blood poisoned so that

their teeth would drop out, and their bones become saturated with virulent scurvy owing to the unwholesome food the law provided they should eat. The hereditary effects of this were in some cases appalling, and yet while this was going on never a voice in the country was raised effectually against it; and if the conditions under which the sailor lives to-day are vastly improved on what they were in the sailing-ship days, he has neither the country nor the Parliament of England to thank for it, but the new class of shipowner who sprang into existence simultaneously with the introduction of steam.

There were many of the old shipowners and shipmasters generous in all their dealings with their men; but my experience compels me to say that a great number of them were heartless skinflints. The economical measures adopted by some captains in order that their supplies might spin out were not only comic, but idiotic. For instance, the master and his chief officer had their meals together, and if they were not on very lovable terms the few minutes allowed the mate was a very monotonous affair owing to the forced and dignified silence of his companion, who eyed with disfavour his healthy appetite; but this did not deter him from continuing to dispose of the meagre repast of vitiated salt junk. The request to be helped a second time broke the silence and brought forth language of a highly improper nature, and did the indiscreet officer happen to boldly go for the butterpot *after* he had partaken of beef he was eloquently reminded that those who "began with beef must finish with beef," and those who "began with butter must finish with butter"! I quote the exact words, for I have heard them. If the mate was of a quarrelsome disposition he retaliated by declaiming against any attempt to restrict his food. Then followed mutual cursings, and hot recriminations. The title of gentleman was repudiated, and "you're another" substituted. But these little squabbles generally passed away without any permanent resentment; and although the mates may have strongly disagreed with the starva-

tion policy of their captains and owners, as soon as they got command themselves they adopted the selfsame methods, and in some cases applied them with a rigour that would have put their former commanders to shame. The scale of provision was a scandal to any civilised nation. Both owners and captains were well aware of this, and shamefully used it as a threat to prevent men from justly complaining of the quality or quantity of food they were being served with. An opportunity was often made so that the men might be put on their "whack," or, to be strictly accurate, the phrase commonly used was "your pound and pint," and as an addendum they were dramatically informed that they should have no fresh provisions in port. The men, of course, naturally retaliated by measuring their work according to the food they got; and then it was seen that the game was to be too costly and too perilous. The common-sense commander would find a judicious retreat from an untenable position, and the blockhead would persevere with it during a whole voyage, and boastfully retail a sickening story of meanness to an audience who, he cherished the idea, would regard him as a hero! How much bitterness and loss was caused by this parochial-minded malignity can never be estimated. It was undoubtedly a prolific factor in making sea-lawyers, and a greater evil than this could not be incubated. The sea-lawyer always was and always will be a pest on land, and a source of mischief and danger on the sea. But while so much can be said against the tactless, and, it may be, the vindictive captain, just as much can be said against some crews who ignored the duty of submitting to control. They feasted on unjustifiable grumbling and discontent. They loafed and plotted to destroy all legitimate authority, and very often made it a perplexity to know how to act towards them. I do not class these men with the criminal class of which I have spoken; there is a very wide distinction between the two. The men I am now speaking of, at their worst, never went beyond loafing, grumbling, and plotting to evade some technical obligation.

The wages of the mate aboard these south-going craft were £5 5s. per month, the second mate got a pound above the A.B.'s, who, on these voyages, were paid £2 10s. to £2 15 s. per month. The cook and steward (one man) got the same as the boatswain, the carpenter, and the second mate. The scale of wages for officers and crew aboard a tea clipper was regulated on more aristocratic lines. Their hands were carefully picked, and, as a rule, they carried double crews, exclusive of officers and petty officers. Both pay and food were vastly better in the clippers than that of the average trader. The statutory scale of provisions was, however, the same for all. A copy of it appears on the opposite page.

SCALE OF PROVISIONS

NOTE.—There is no scale fixed by the Board of Trade. The quantity and nature of the Provisions are a matter for agreement between Master and Crew.

Scale of Provisions to be allowed and served out to the Crew during the Voyage, in
addition to the daily issue of Lime and Lemon Juice and Sugar, or other Anti-Scorbutics in any case required by the Act.

PROVISIONS.	QUANTITY	SUN.	MON.	TUE.	WED.	THUR.	FRI.	SAT.	WEEKLY
Water	Qts.	3	3	3	3	3	3	3	
Bread	lb.	1	1	1	1	1	1	1	
Beef	"	1-1/2		1-1/2		1-1/2		1-1/2	
Pork	"		1-1/4		1-1/4		1-1/4		
Preserved Meats	"								
Preserved Potatoes	oz.								
Preserved Vegetables.	lb.								
Flour	"	1/2		1/2		1/2		1/2	
Peas	Pint	1/3		1/3		1/3		1/3	
Calavances	"								
Rice	lb.								
Oatmeal	"								1/2
Barley	"								
Salted Fish	"								
Condensed Milk	oz.								
Tea	"	1/8	1/8	1/8	1/8	1/8	1/8	1/8	
Coffee Beans (Roasted)	"	1/2	1/2	1/2	1/2	1/2	1/2	1/2	
Cocoa	"								
Sugar	"	2	2	2	2	2	2	2	
Dried Fruit (Raisins, Currants, &c.)	"								
Butter	lb.								
Marmalade or Jam	"								
Molasses	Pint								
Mustard	oz.								
Pepper	"								
Vinegar or Pickles	Pint								

[1] . .

. .

SUBSTITUTES AND EQUIVALENTS.

Equivalent Substitutes at the Master's option. No spirits allowed.

FOOTNOTES:

[1] Other articles may be inserted here.

CHAPTER VIII

LIFE AMONG THE PACKET RATS

It is a noteworthy fact that many of the featherbrained, harum-scarum captains endeavoured to man their vessels with men who had been trained in north-country colliers. These men were considered not only the best, but the most subordinate in the world. Perhaps this was correct, but I think the west countrymen could claim a good place in point of seamanship, if not of subordination. I remember hearing the captain of an Australian passenger vessel making this complimentary statement of north-country men to my father, when I was a very small boy, and I learnt by experience many years afterwards that it was true. Life aboard some of the packet ships was a chronic convulsion of devilry. The majority of the men constituting the crew were termed "packet rats," and were the scrapings of British and foreign scoundrelism. No wonder the captains were anxious to have a proportion of fine, able-bodied north-country sailors, as a steadying influence on the devil-may-care portion of the crew. The signing on of a packet ship was quite an historic occasion. All the "gimlet-eyed" rascals in town were on the alert to bleed the sailor as soon as he had got his advance. It was usual for the sailors to sign articles binding themselves to be aboard at 5.30 or 6 a.m. on a fixed date, and in order that there might be no mistake as to how the discipline of the vessel was to be administered, the officers, who were generally Yankees, or aped the habits and manners of the Yankee, were stationed at the gangways for the purpose of suitably receiving the wretched, drink-sodden, semi-delirious creatures who were to constitute part of the crew. They were carted to the vessel, accompanied by animals opprobriously called "crimps," whose unrestrained appetite for plunder was a scandal to the public authority who permitted their existence. After these noxious gentry had sucked the blood of their victims, the latter were handed over to the officers who awaited their arrival at the gangway. Having arrived late, and in a condition contrary to the orthodox opinions of their officer, they were asked in strong nasal language why they did not turn up at 6 a.m.

"Do you know," the slap-dashing mate would say, "that you have committed a breach of discipline that cannot be overlooked on this craft?"

The half-drunken, whiskey-soaked creature would reply in an incoherent, semi-insolent way, whereupon the mate would haul out a belaying pin and belabour him with it. Many a criminal act of this kind was committed, and if the men as a body retaliated, they were shot at, or knuckle-dustered, until their faces and bodies were beaten into a pulp. This was called mutiny; so in addition to being brutally maltreated, there could be found, both at home and abroad, gentlemen in authority who had them sent to prison, and who confiscated their pay. Many of them were punished until they agreed to sign the entry in the official log against themselves.

It may be thought that these officers were justified in the initial stages of the voyage in striking terror into the minds of these men, so that their criminal instincts might be kept in check. I am well aware of the risks and responsibilities attending the control of a terrible class of persons such as the American "packet rat," and it is difficult to write of them with calmness of judgment. They were undoubtedly collections of incorrigible ruffians such as could not have been easily employed in any other class of British or American vessel. At the same time, it must be remembered that the officers of these crafts were not selected because of their pre-disposition to piety. It was because of their predilection for living in a chronic atmosphere of "Almighty Hell." They were trained to it, and were apt pupils. They saw a glory in the continuity of combat that raged from the beginning until the end of a voyage. It is worthy of note that, with few exceptions, they never allowed themselves to be overcome, though many a futile attempt was made. Poor devils of sailors! Many a voyage they made without receiving a penny for it, every cent of their wages being confiscated in fines and forfeitures. How many may have lost their lives during the progress of such passages, ostensibly by accidentally falling overboard, will never be known. I have heard old salts talk of these vessels never being hove to to pick up any of the unfortunate riff-raff who may have made a false step into the ocean. This may or may not be true; but from what I know of the desperate character of those commanders and officers, I am inclined to give credence to a good deal of what is said to have occurred.

The really first-class seamen on these vessels (both American and British) were treated not only with fairness, but very often with indulgence. It was not unusual, however, for them to have to fight their way to having proper respect paid to them. The expert seaman, who could box as well as he could handle a marline spike or use a sail-needle, appealed to the sympathies of the captain and officers. It must not be supposed that either the officers or men who were thought good enough to sail in these vessels were in any degree representative of the great bulk of British captains, officers, or men. At the same time, I do not mean to suggest that the rest of the mercantile marine was, or ever could be, composed of Puritans. But the men I have been trying to describe were the very antithesis of the typical British tar. Many of them were, constitutionally, criminals, who had spent years compulsorily on the Spanish main, when not undergoing punishment in prison. Having been shipmate with some of them I am able to speak of their character with some claim to authority. They were big bullies, and consequently abject cowards. The tales I have heard them relate before and during their sojourn on the Spanish main reeked with a villainous odour. They always commenced their bullying tactics as soon as they came aboard, especially if the vessel had apparently a quiet set of officers and a peaceful captain. They did not always gauge aright the pugilistic capacity of some of their forecastle brethren, and so it came to pass that once one of these six-feet-four rampaging creatures was threatening annihilation to a little forecastle colony, and, indeed, to the after-end colonists also, when there was heard, amid a flow of sulphurous curses, a quiet, defiant word of disapproval. It came from a Scottish able seaman who had served long in American sailing vessels. The orator promptly struck out at the semi-inanimate Sandy, who woke up, went for his man in true British style, and had him howling for mercy in less than two minutes. The Scottish sailor became the idol of the captain and crew, and the Yankee bullies deserted at the first port the vessel touched at. In 1871 I shipped aboard a barque in Liverpool as chief officer. I was very young, and what perhaps was more sinful, very youthful looking. The captain was only two years my senior, and the second mate four. There was a scarcity of desirable men available, which resulted in our having to engage what we could get, and, with the exception of three respectable men, the rest were "packet rats," though few of them had sailed in packets, and those who had were stamped with the mark of it. We left Birkenhead in tow. There was a strong wind blowing. It was my duty to see the anchors stowed properly. I gave orders to man the fish tackle, and directed one of the men to pinch the flukes of the anchor on to the gunwale while the crew were hauling on the tackle. He looked at me for a minute or two as though he were undecided as to the condition of his hearing and his eyesight. I repeated the order in authoritative quarter-deck style. He gaped in amazement apparently at my audacity, and told me in language that could not be overlooked there (or repeated here!) to do myself what I had ordered him to do. I became at once conscious of my youthful appearance! I assured him that I would stand no nonsense, and perhaps to awaken him to the possibilities of a physical encounter, I used some Americanisms that were obviously familiar to him and to the others who were ready to act with him. I insisted that the orders I had given should be carried out. He sneered at my youth, and intimated, with a grin that foreboded cannibalism, that he had eaten many a more manly-looking person than myself before breakfast, and that he would stand no G—— d—— cheek from a son of a— — like me! "Do it yourself," said he, "I won't," and suiting the action to the words, he tossed the handspike on to the top-gallant forecastle. I instantly picked it up, and it was all over his body before he had time to recover from the effect of so sudden an attack. The captain had told me that I was to beware of treachery, and to remember the advantage of the first blow. "Hit," said he, "right between the eyes, and see to it that it makes sparks!" I did not expect that the necessity would arise so soon after leaving the docks, and I must plead guilty to inaccurately carrying out the captain's suggestion, except in so far as the first blow was concerned, which was quickly and decisively struck, although not precisely between the eyes. There were visible signs that the head and face of the rebel had sustained damage; and it may be taken for granted that other parts of his body did not escape. He intimated that for the present he wanted no more, and I was secretly glad of it because I had been severely punished myself, although my general appearance did not show it much. Surely the only course open to me after so unjustifiable an attack was to resent not only the insubordination, but the filthy personal attack on myself. We had not arrived at the N. W. lightship where the tug was to cast off the tow-rope when this rebellion began, and it continued more or less until the vessel arrived at her destination, where the whole of the refractory ones were put in prison and kept there until she was ready to sail. They were then brought aboard by police escort. Prison diet and prison treatment had knocked a lot of the fight out of them, but the ship food soon revived the devil in them again. We had not been at sea many days before they commenced to revolt even against steering and making or shortening sail. It was only by the application of stringent measures that they were kept in subjection. It was found necessary for the captain and officers not only to lock their state-room doors when in bed, but to keep themselves well armed in case of a sudden rising. The suspense of it was terrible. We knew that a slight relaxation in the stern disciplinary attitude might give them an opportunity which they would be quick to take advantage of; it was therefore resolutely adhered to. The captain instilled into his officers the doctrine of keeping them always at work, bad weather or fine. "Make them permanently tired," said he; "make them feel fit for their bunks." That was all very well, but in order to carry this out the officers were kept permanently tired also.

Though many years have elapsed since those troubled days and nights, the memory of them is still with me, watching, working, wakeful, always on the alert, anticipating assassination; even my brief sleep was troubled with visions of sanguinary conflict. It was no mere delusion. Each day brought evidences of coming trouble. How and when it would come did not matter, so long as we were prepared for it. Whisperings and audible grumblings were ominous tokens of what was in the wind. The captain and I had some conversation concerning the situation. He was of opinion that the sailor who opened the rebellion at the beginning of the voyage would lead an open and concerted revolt, and perhaps I agreed with him that something of the sort might easily happen; so we resolved to keep a tight eye on this sinister development. One night about ten o'clock, while beating through a narrow channel, the captain said to me, "I am going below; you must take charge." And after giving me the necessary instructions, he said in a low tone, "Now mind, keep your eyes and ears wide open; you may be taken unawares at any moment." I thanked him for the advice, and he bade me goodnight and left the poop. An Irishman was at the wheel, and for a time his steering was good. As the wind was dead in our teeth and blowing strong, the course was full and by the wind. It soon became necessary to tack, and as it is always customary for the officer in charge to take the helm in performing this evolution, it became my duty to do so, but as soon as the vessel was round, I told the man to take the wheel again. I then proceeded to see that all the sails were properly trimmed. This being done, I went on to the poop again, and as the helmsman was steering in a most erratic fashion, first sailing her bang off the wind and then shaking the sails almost aback, I remonstrated with him, but to no purpose. At last I said to him that if he did not steer better, I would be obliged to turn him from the wheel. No greater disgrace can be inflicted on a self-respecting seaman than this. I have known men suffer an agony by the mere threat of it. But the heterogeneous crew that we had to control had no sensitiveness of that kind. I was told, amid a running stream of filthy swearing, to take the wheel myself. The ship and all in authority were cursed with Hibernian fluency. A special appeal was made for our immediate consignment to the hottest part of hell. The harangue was suddenly cut short by my jumping from the poop on top of him as he was about to pass away from the helm. I had ordered a hand whom I could trust to steer, while I became engaged in physically reproving this blackguard for his insolence and disobedience to lawful commands. During my struggle with him I felt a sharp prick as though a pin had been run into me, but owing to the excitement of the moment I took no further notice of it—indeed, I was too busy to notice anything. The job did not prove so difficult as I had anticipated. His accomplices did not come to his assistance, and he evidently lost heart and became effusively submissive. The captain relieved me at midnight, and I returned to my berth. I was awakened during the watch by some one tapping at my door. It turned out to be the captain. When I admitted him he showed me a knife which he had picked up on the deck, and asked if I knew whom it belonged to. I said "Yes, it belongs to the Irishman." "Well," said he, "it was evidently his intention to bleed you." I was sitting up in my bunk, and suddenly observed a clot of blood on my shirt, and said to him, "I have been stabbed. Look at this." I examined myself, and found a slight cut where I had felt the sensation which I have spoken of. We conferred as to whether he should be put in irons, and given up to the authorities at the first port the vessel touched at. I asked to be allowed to deal with him when he came on deck, and it was agreed that I should. He was in due course ordered aft, and the knife shown to him. When asked if it was his, he became afflicted with fear, and admitted that he had attempted to stab me, and begged that he should not be further punished, and if he were allowed to resume his duty he promised with emotional profusion to give no further annoyance to any one. The appeal was pathetic; it would have been an act of vindictive cruelty not to have granted what he asked; though his conduct in conjunction with the others had up to that time been vicious in the extreme. It was thought desirable to give his promises a test, with the result that he gave no outward signs of violating them while the voyage lasted.

These men were mutineers by profession. Sentiment, or what is called moral suasion, was unintelligible to them. They were a species of wild beast that could only be tamed by the knowledge that they were weaker than the power set over them; and this could only be conveyed in one way that was understandable to them: that is, by coming down to their level for the time being, and smashing their courage (and their heads if need be) with electrical suddenness. If there was any hesitation, depend upon it they would smash you. The moralist will declaim against the adoption of such a doctrine, and will bring theoretic arguments in support of his theories; but before commencing a tirade against an unavoidable method, perhaps the moralist will state whether he has ever been confronted with a situation which might involve not only the unlawful absorption of supreme control, but the sacrifice of life and valuable property as a consequence of it. Let me put this proposition to them. Here is a vessel, it may be, out on a trackless ocean hundreds of miles from land, her forecastle hands consisting of a gang of murderous ruffians ready to make lawful authority impotent, and, if need be, to enforce their own by overpowering the captain and officers and making an opportunity for mutiny. Let the moralists think of it; four or five men at the mercy of a score of hang-dog scoundrels who despise every moral law, and who talk lightly of murder and every form of violent death! Let me ask them what their feelings would be suppose any of their near relations were placed in the position of having to fight for lawful supremacy and even for life? I think this might be trying to their faith in theoretic and sentimental government. But the question might be made more impressive still by devoting a chapter to the hideous butchery which horrified creation when the news came of the mutiny of the *Flowery Land* and the *Caswell*. I should like people who are so deadly virtuous as to repudiate self-preservation to picture the decks of these two vessels washed in human blood, and to imagine (if it is not too dreadful to do so) that some of it belonged to a kinsman who was very dear to them. I think if they are not past praying for they would then give up dispensing cant, and direct their sympathies to a policy that has the merit of being not only humane but logical. I well know how narrow the dividing line is between proper and improper discipline; and know also the care that should be used in such circumstances to act with fairness and even kindness. But I am writing about a section of men who mistake kindness for weakness, and who can only be appealed to and swayed by the magic of fear. I could find material to fill a three-hundred page book with the experiences of that one eventful and hazardous voyage. Space forbids my giving more than a brief account of it.

After ten months' absence from Liverpool we arrived at Antwerp. The conduct of some of the crew had been so shocking that they feared the penalty of it, and they absconded immediately on arrival, and were never heard of by us again. The Irishman fulfilled his pledge so thoroughly that he was not only pardoned but kept by the vessel. The more defiant of them saw the thing through, and received only a portion of their wages, the bulk of it being deducted for fines and forfeitures. I am bound to say these men got what they richly deserved. They had on several occasions endangered the safety of a handsome and valuable vessel and the lives of all aboard. But for the loyalty of the petty officers and the unyielding firmness of a strong, capable captain underwriters would have had a heavy loss to pay for.

The tale I have been unfolding shows one unwholesome and vicious aspect of sailor life. There is, happily, a more attractive, peaceful, and manifestly brighter and purer aspect; and those who live in it are beloved by every one.

CHAPTER IX

BRUTALITY AT SEA

In those days the deep-sea shipmaster looked upon the collier skipper as his inferior in everything, and regarded himself in the light of an important personage. His bearing was that of a man who believed that he was sent into the world so that great deeds might be accomplished. He lavishly patronised everybody, and never disguised his desire to repudiate all connection with his less imposing fellow-worker in a different sphere. He would pace the poop or quarter-deck of his vessel with the air of a monarch. Sometimes a slight omission of deference to his monarchy would take place on the part of officers or crew. That was an infringement of dignity which had to be promptly reproved by stern disciplinary measures.

There were various methods open to him of inflicting chastisement. An offending officer was usually ordered to his berth for twenty-four hours—that is put off duty. The seamen's offences were rigorously atoned for by their being what is called "worked up," *i.e.,* kept on duty during their watch below; or, what was more provoking still, they might be ordered to "sweat up" sails that they knew did not require touching. This idle aggravation was frequently carried out with the object of getting the men to revolt; they were then logged for refusing duty and their pay stopped at the end of the voyage. It was not an infrequent occurrence for grown men to be handcuffed for some minor offence that should never have been noticed. The sight of human suffering and degradation was an agreeable excitement to this class of officer or captain. If some of the villainy committed in the name of the law at sea were to be written, it would be a revolting revelation of wickedness, of unheard-of cruelty. Small cabin-boys who had not seen more than twelve summers were good sport for frosty-blooded scoundrels to rope's-end or otherwise brutally use, because they failed to do their part in stowing a royal or in some other way showed indications of limited strength or lack of knowledge. The barbarous creed of the whole class was to lash their subjects to their duties. A little fellow, well known to myself, who had not reached his thirteenth year, had his eyes blacked and his little body scandalously maltreated because he had been made nervous by continuous bullying, and did not steer so well as he might have done had he been left alone. It is almost incredible, but it is true, some of these rascals would at times have men hung up by their thumbs in the mizen rigging for having committed what would be considered nowadays a most trivial offence.

One gentleman, well known in his time by the name of Bully W——, stood on the poop of the square-rigged ship *Challenge*, and *shot* a seaman who was at work on the main yardarm! It was never known precisely why he did it; but it was well known that had he not made his exit from the cabin windows, and had he not received assistance to escape, he would have been lynched by a furious public. This man once commanded a crack, square-rigged clipper called the *Flying Cloud*. His passages between New York and San Francisco were a marvel to everybody. He was credited, as many others like him have been, with having direct communication with the devil, and is said never to have voluntarily taken canvas in. He was one of those who used to lock tacks and sheets, so that if the officers were overcome by fear they could not shorten canvas. His fame spread until it was considered an honour to look upon him, much less to know him. He became the object of adoration, and perhaps his knowledge of this swelled his conceit, so that he came to believe that even the shooting of his seamen was not a murderous, but a permissible act, so far as *he* was concerned. But this man was only one among scores like him.

There was once a famous captain of a well-known Australian clipper, a slashing, dare-devil fellow, who made the quickest passages to and from Australia on record. But at last he lost his head, and then of course his money, and died in very pinched circumstances. Poor fellow, he couldn't stand corn! The people of Liverpool gave a banquet in honour of him. He arrived late in the banqueting hall, and there were indications that he was inebriated. When he had to respond to the toast of his health he shocked his audience by stating that he

would either be in hell or in Melbourne in so many days from the time of sailing. Destiny ordained that he was not to be in hell, and not in Melbourne either—only hard and fast on Australian rocks! His misfortunes and his habits soon put an end to his professional career, but his deeds are deservedly talked of to this day. He was undoubtedly one of the smartest men of his time, and ought to have been saved from the end that befell him.

Captains who claimed public attention for reasons that would not now be looked upon with favour were usually known by the opprobrious name of "Bully this" or "Bully that;" but "Jack the Devil" and "Hell Fire Jack" were perhaps as widely used names as any others. There were various causes for the acquisition of such distinction. It was generally the fearless way in which they carried sail, and their harsh, brutal treatment of their crews that fixed the epithet upon them. I am quite sure many of them were proud of it. They were conscious of having done something to deserve it. It will appear strange that seamen should have been found to sail with such commanders; not only could they be found, but many were even eager to sail with them, the reason being that they desired to share some of the notoriety which their captains had acquired. They loved to talk of having sailed in a vessel made famous by the person who commanded her, even if he were a bully! His heroics were made an everlasting theme. The A.B.s rarely made more than one voyage with him; many of them deserted even at the first port. The dreadful usage, and the fear of being killed or drowned, were too much for them sometimes.

CHAPTER X

BRAVERY

Amid the many sides of the average sailor's character there is none that stands out so prominently as that of bravery and resourcefulness. Here is an instance of both qualities. Three or four years ago a Russian Nihilist made his escape from the Siberian mines and travelled to Vladivostock. A British

ship was lying there, and the poor refugee came aboard and claimed the protection of her captain. The vessel could not sail for a few days, which gave his pursuers an opportunity of overtaking him. They got to know where he was, and proceeded to demand that he should be given up. They relied, as many other whipper-snappers do, on the importance of their official position and the glitter of their elaborate uniform to strike awe and terror into the soul of the British captain! They soon found out what a mistake they had made. "Gentlemen," said the resolute commander, "the person whom you call your prisoner has placed himself under the protection of the British flag. A British ship is British territory, hence he is a free man, and I must request that you cease to molest us or make any attempt to take him by force." They urged Imperial penalties and international complications; but this brave and resourceful man disregarded their threats, again reminding them that he stood on the deck of a British vessel; and that if they did anything in violation of his power and authority, complications would arise from his side instead of from theirs. He was allowed to sail with his interesting passenger aboard, and I hope the latter was genuinely grateful to his heroic protector for ever after. The name of such a man should be covered with imperishable fame.

A PARTING CHEER TO THE OUTWARD BOUND

Here is another bit of quiet bravery, loftier than the slaughter, in hot or cold blood, of one's fellow-creatures! About twenty-eight or twenty-nine years ago, a German vessel ran into and sank off Dungeness an emigrant ship called the *North Fleet*. She was a fine vessel. Her commander had married a young lady a few days before sailing from London, and she accompanied him on the voyage. When the collision occurred there was a rush made for the boats. Men clamoured for a place to the exclusion of women and children! The captain called out that he would shoot the first man who prevented or did not assist the women to save themselves, and I believe he had reason to put his threat into practice. He stood on the poop with his revolver in hand ready for action. When the proper time came, he asked his bride to take his arm, and led her to the gangway. They kissed each other affectionately. He whispered in her ear, "Courage, dear, I must do my duty." Then he handed her into the boat which was in charge of an officer, and exhorted him to take special care of her whom he had so recently led from the altar and to whom he had said his last farewell! He then proceeded to his post on the quarter-deck, and stood there until the vessel sank and the sea flowed over him. The opinion at the time was that he could have saved his life if he had made an effort to do so. I question this very much, as many of the people were picked up in the water, clinging to wreckage; the boats being overcrowded. The only way by which he could have been saved was to displace some one or clutch at a piece of wreck. He preferred death to the former, and there is no evidence that he did not attempt to save himself by means of the latter. The probability is that he gave any such opportunity to some drowning man or woman, and sacrificed himself. Honour to this brave man who died, not while taking life, but in saving it!

CHAPTER XI

CHANTIES

The signing on and the sailing from Liverpool or London docks of these vessels were not only exciting but pathetic occasions. The chief officer usually had authority to pick the crew. The men would be brought into the yard and formed into line. The chanty-man was generally the first selection, and care was taken that the balance should be good choristers, and that all were able to produce good discharges for conduct and ability. It was a great sight to see the majestic-looking vessels sail away. The dock walls would be crowded with sympathetic audiences who had come not only to say farewell, but to listen to the sweet though sombre refrain that charged the air with the enchanting pathos and beauty of "Goodbye, fare you well." The like of it has never been heard since those days. Attempts have been made to reproduce the original, and have failed. Nobody can reproduce anything like it, because it is a gift exclusively the sailors' own, and the charm filled the soul with delightful emotions that caught you like a strong wind.

The chanty-man was a distinguished person whom it was impolitic to ignore. He was supposed to combine the genius of a musical prodigy and an impromptu poet! If his composition was directed to any real or even imaginary grievances, it was always listened to by sensible captains and officers without showing any indications of ill-humour. Indeed, I have seen captains laugh very heartily at these exquisite comic thrusts which were intended to shape the policy of himself and his officers towards the crew. If the captain happened to be a person of no humour and without the sense of music this method of conveyance was abortive, but it went on all the same until nature forced a glimpse into his hazy mind of what it all meant! Happily there are few sailors who inherit such a defective nature. It is a good thing that some of these thrilling old songs have been preserved to us. Even if they do not convey an accurate impression of the sailors' way of rendering them, they give some faint idea of it. The complicated arrangement of words in some of the songs is without parallel in their peculiar jargon, and yet there are point and intention evident throughout them. For setting sail, "Blow, boys, blow" was greatly favoured, and its quivering, weird air had a wild fascination in it. "Boney was a warrior" was singularly popular, and was nearly always sung in hoisting the topsails. The chanty-man would sit on the topsail halyard block and sing the solo, while the choristers rang out with touching beauty the chorus, at the same time giving two long, strong pulls on the halyards. This song related mainly to matters of history, and was sung with a rippling tenderness which seemed to convey that the singers' sympathies were with the Imperial martyr who was kidnapped into exile and to death by a murderous section of the British aristocracy. The soloist warbled the great Emperor's praises, and portrayed him as having affinity to the godlike. His death was proclaimed as the most atrocious crime committed since the Crucifixion, and purgatory was assigned as a fitting repository for the souls of his mean executioners. The words of these songs may be distressing jargon, but the refrain as sung by the seamen was very fine to listen to:—

HAUL THE BOWLING (SETTING SAIL)

Haul th' bowlin', the fore and maintack bowlin',
Haul th' bowlin', the bowlin' haul!
Haul th' bowlin', the skipper he's a-growlin',
Haul th' bowlin', the bowlin' haul.
Haul th' bowlin', oh Kitty is me darlin',
Haul th' bowlin', the bowlin' haul.
Haul th' bowlin', the packet is a bowlin';
Haul th' bowlin', the bowlin' haul.

As for the song itself, it was as follows:—

BONEY WAS A WARRIOR

Oh, Boney was a Corsican,
Oh aye oh,
Oh, Boney was a Corsican,
John France wa! (François.)
But Boney was a warrior,
Oh aye oh,
But Boney was a warrior,
John France wa.
Oh, Boney licked the Austrians!—
Oh aye oh,
Oh, Boney licked the Austrians!—
John France wa!
The Russians and the Prussians!
Oh aye oh,
The Russians and the Prussians!
John France wa.

Five times he entered Vienna!
Oh aye oh,
Five times he entered Vienna,
John France wa.
He married an Austrian princess,
Oh aye oh,
He married an Austrian princess,
John France wa.
Then he marched on Moscow,
Oh aye oh,
Then he marched on Moscow,
John France wa.
But Moscow was a-blazing!
Oh aye oh,
But Moscow was a-blazing,
John France wa.
Then Boney he retreated,
Oh aye oh,
Then Boney he retreated,
John France wa.
Boney went to Waterloo,
Oh aye oh,
Boney went to Waterloo,
John France wa.
And Boney was defeated,
Oh aye oh,
And Boney was defeated,
John France wa.
Oh Boney's made a prisoner,
Oh aye oh,
Oh Boney's made a prisoner,
John France wa.
They sent him to St. Helena!
Oh aye oh,
They sent him to St. Helena,
John France wa!
Oh Boney was ill-treated!
Oh aye oh,
Oh Boney was ill-treated,
John France wa!
Oh Boney's heart was broken!
Oh aye oh,
Oh Boney's heart was broken,
John France wa.
Oh Boney died a warrior;—
Oh aye oh,
Oh Boney died a warrior,
John France wa.
But Boney was an Emperor!
Oh aye oh!
But Boney was an Emperor,
John France wa!

This song never failed to arouse the greatest enthusiasm, so much so that the officer in charge had to keep a keen eye on what was going on and shout out "belay!" before something should be broken! The sailors' regard for the great Emperor was a passion; and as they neared the final tragedy they seemed to imagine they were in combat with his foes, so that it was dangerous to leave them without strict supervision.

One of the most rollicking and joyous days the sailor had during a voyage was that on which his dead horse expired; that is, when his month's advance was worked out. If he took a month's advance, he always considered that he had worked that month for nothing: and, literally, he had done so, as the money given to him in advance usually went towards paying a debt or having a spree; so it was fitting, considering these circumstances, that special recognition should be made of the arrival of such a period. An improvised horse was therefore constructed, and a block with a rope rove through it was hooked on to the main yardarm. The horse was bent on, and the ceremony commenced by leading the rope to the winch or capstan, and the song entitled "The Dead Horse" was sung with great gusto. The funeral procession as a rule was spun out a long time, and when the horse was allowed to arrive at the yard arm the rope was slipped and he fell into the sea amid much hilarity! The verse which announces his death was as follows:—

"They say my horse is dead and gone;—
And they say so, and they say so!
They say my horse is dead and gone;—
Oh, poor old man!"

The verse which extinguishes him by dropping him into the sea goes like this:—

"Then drop him to the depths of the sea;—
And they say so, and they say so!
Then drop him to the depths of the sea;—
Oh, poor old man!"

This finished the important event of the voyage; then began many pledges of thrift to be observed for evermore, which were never kept longer than the arrival at the next port, or at the longest until the arrival at a home port, when restraint was loosened. The same old habits were resumed, and the same old month's advance was required before sailing on another voyage.

The "White Stocking Day" was as great an event ashore as the Dead Horse day was at sea. The sailors' wives, mothers, or sweethearts always celebrated half-pay day by wearing white stockings and by carrying their skirts discreetly high enough so that it might be observed. This custom was carried out with rigid regularity, and the participators were the objects of sympathetic attraction. Poor things, there is no telling what it cost them in anxiety to keep it up. Their half-pay would not exceed thirty shillings per month, and they had much to do with it, besides providing white stockings and a suitable rig to grace the occasion.

"We're homeward bound and I hear the sound," was the favourite song when heaving up the anchor preparatory to pointing homeward. This chanty has a silken, melancholy, and somewhat soft breeziness about it, and when it was well sung its flow went fluttering over the harbour, which re-echoed the joyous tidings until soloist and choristers alike became entranced by the power of their own performances; and the multitudes who on these occasions came to listen did not escape the rapture of the fleeting throbs of harmony which charged the atmosphere, and made you feel that you would like to live under such sensations for ever!

HOMEWARD BOUND (HEAVING THE ANCHOR)

Our anchor's a-weigh and our sails are well set;—
Goodbye, fare you well; goodbye, fare you well!
And the friends we are leaving we leave with
regret;—
Hurrah! my boys, we're homeward bound!
We're homeward bound, and I hear the sound;—
Goodbye, fare you well; goodbye, fare you well!
Come, heave on the cable and make it spin round!—
Hurrah! my boys, we're homeward

bound!
Oh let ourselves go, and heave long and
strong;—
Goodbye, fare you well; goodbye, fare
you well!
Sing then the chorus for 'tis a good
song;—
Hurrah! my boys, we're homeward
bound!
We're homeward bound you've heard
me say;—
Goodbye, fare you well; goodbye, fare
you well!
Hook on the cat-fall, and then run away!
Hurrah! my boys, we're homeward
bound!

After a long, dreary pilgrimage of trackless oceans, the last chant had to be sung
as their vessel was being warped
through the docks to her discharging
berth; and now all their grievances,
joys, and sorrows were poured forth in
"Leave her, Johnnie, leave her!" It was
their last chance of publicly announcing
approval or disapproval of their ship,
their captain, and their treatment. Here
is a sample of it:—

"I thought I heard the skipper say,
'Leave her, Johnnie, leave her!
To-morrow you will get your pay,
Leave her, Johnnie, leave her!'
The work was hard, the voyage was
long;—
Leave her, Johnnie, leave her!
The seas were high, the gales were
strong;—
It's time for us to leave her!
The food was bad, the wages low;—
Leave her, Johnnie, leave her!
But now ashore again we'll go;—
It's time for us to leave her!
The sails are furled, our work is done!
Leave her, Johnnie, leave her!
And now on shore we'll have our fun!
It's time for us to leave her! &c, &c."

Such songs were not stereotyped in their
composition. They varied according to
circumstances. Sometimes they were
denunciatory, and at other times full of
fun, praise of the ship, and pathos.
There was seldom a middle course, but
whatever side was taken the sponta-
neous poetic effusion was not ended until the whole story had been unfolded.

CHAPTER XII

JACK IN RATCLIFF HIGHWAY

As soon as the vessel was moored
in a home port, decks cleared up and
washed down, the mate intimated to the
crew that their services would not be required any longer; and those who wanted it, received a portion of the balance
of wages due to them in advance until
they signed clear of the articles. There
were few who did not take advantage of
this, and many of them had disbursed it
in one way or another long before the
three days' grace, which was allowed
the captain to make up his accounts and
pay off, had expired.

The villainous agencies at work in
those days (and even in these) to decoy
poor Jack, could be counted by the
score. Their task was not a difficult one.
They knew him to be a complacent prey
for their plans to drug and rob him.
Many of these poor fellows on the first
night after landing would allow the
whole of a voyage's earnings to be
bartered from them, so that before they
actually received their balance of wages
they had spent it, and they became
ready for the first ship, which oft-times,
indeed, was long in turning up. Mean-
while they were turned into the street
without any compunction, just as they
stood. Of course they were to blame;
but what about the evil tribe who tempted them? They should have been made
to refund every penny that had been ex-
torted while their victims were under
the influence of drink, or should have
been made to do six months in lieu of
refunding. This plan might be adopted
with advantage to the community even
at the present time.

In these sailor circles there was once
a well-known incorrigible named Jimmie Hall, a native of Blyth, who for the
most part sailed out of London on long
voyages. It did not matter how long
Jimmie had been away on a voyage, or
how much pay he had to take, he was
never longer than a week in funds, and
more frequently only one or two days.
This half-tamed creature was walking
up Ratcliffe Highway one winter morning between two and three o'clock, and
he met an old shipmate of his. They

greeted each other with some warmth.
Jimmie's friend related to him a tale of
destitution. He had been on the spree,
spent all his money, and two days before had been turned out of the boarding
house, and had slept out for two nights.
Jimmie, with sailor-like generosity,
said, "I am glad to have met you. It
gives me an opportunity of asking you
to share with me rooms at my hotel."

"Hotel!" gasped the bewildered shipmate. "Have you had money left you?
You always were a good sort."

"No," said his companion; "I have
had no money left me, but I thought I
would stay in an hotel this time. I can go
out and in whenever I like, and I find it
an advantage to do so. The doors are always open. Come along!"

The two friends walked up the highway arm in arm, Jimmie observing a pa-
tronising silence while his companion
covered him with affectionate compli-
ments. After they had walked a considerable distance in meditation, the shipmate said—

"Where is the hotel? Are we far off?"

"No," said the accommodating Jimmie; "here it is. I must make one condition with you before we get any nearer.
You must go in by the back door."

"I will go in by any b—— door you
like. I am not a particular chap in that
way!"

"Very well," said Jimmie, pointing to
an object in the middle of the road;
"then you go in there, and I will go in by
the front."

"But," said his shipmate, "that is a
boiler."

"*You*" said the philanthropic James,
"may call it what you like, but, for the
time being, it is my hotel! It has been
my residence for two weeks, and I offer
you the end I do not use. If you accept
it, all that you require to make you perfectly comfortable is a bundle of straw.
We shall sit rent free!"

Needless to say the offer was accepted, and the two "plants" lived together
until they got a ship.

Mr. Hall's knowledge of the Highway, as it was called, enabled him to
be of occasional service to the police,
hence he was on the most cordial terms

of friendship with them. He could swoop plain-clothes men through intricacies which flashed with the flames of crime, without exciting the slightest suspicion of the object he had in view. He could talk, swear, and drink in accurate harmony with his acquaintances, and was looked upon with favour by a circle of estimable friends. Members of the constabulary were always considerate and accommodating towards him during his periodic outbursts of alcoholic craving. He owed much to the care they took of him during his fits of debauchery; and he was not unmindful of it when he had the wherewithal to compensate them. Like most of those wayward inebriates who followed the sea as a calling, he was a perfect sailor; and even his capricious sensual habits did not prevent him being sought to rejoin vessels he had sailed in.

Jimmie Hall was only one among thousands of fine fellows who were encouraged to go to bestial excesses by gangs of predatory vermin (men and women) who infested Wapping and Ratcliffe Highway.

There was a tradition amongst sailors, which I am inclined to give some credence to, that a certain barber who had a shop in the Highway availed himself of the opportunity, while cutting the hair or shaving his sailor customers—mainly, it was thought, those who were sodden with drink—to sever their wind-pipe, rob them of all they had, and then pull the bolt of a carefully concealed trap-door which communicated with the Thames, and drop their weighted bodies out of sight! This system of sanguinary murder is supposed to have been carried on for some years, until a sailor of great physical power, suspecting foul play to some of his pals, went boldly in, was politely asked to take his seat, and assumed a drunken attitude which caused the barber to think he had an easy victim. The barber wormed his way into Jack's confidence, who was very communicative as to the length of his voyage and the amount of money he had been paid off with. He flattered him with loving profusion, and was about to take the razor up and com-

mence his deadly work, when the sailor, who had discerned the secret trap, jumped up, pulled a revolver from his pocket, and demanded that the trap-door should be shown to him, or his brains would be scattered all over the place! The barber implored that his life should be spared, and piteously denied the existence of a secret communication with the river. Jack's attitude was threatening; the supplicant pleaded that if his life was spared he would do what was asked of him. The condition was agreed on, and the trap opened. It disclosed a liquid vault. The sailor accused the panic-stricken villain of foul murder, and of having this place as a repository for his unsuspecting victims, and the man shrieked alternate incoherent denials and confessions. The sailor suspected the awful truth all along, but now he became satisfied of it, and forcing the barber towards the vault, he ordered him to jump down; he had to choose between this and being shot. He preferred the former mode of extinction, so plunged in. The hatch was then covered over him, and there were no more murders.

RATCLIFF HIGHWAY: "CARRYING SMALL CANVAS"

Another of the many instances of the resourceful mariner's irrepressible gaiety even under most embarrassing conditions is contained in a story which I heard related aboard ship in the early days of my sea-life many times, and the veracity of it was always vouched for by the narrator whose personal acquaintance with the gentlemen concerned was an indispensable factor in the interest of the tale, and a distinction he was proud of to a degree. I have said that Ratcliffe Highway was the rendezvous of seafaring men. It provided them with a wealth of facilities for the expeditious disposal of money that had been earned at great hazard, and not infrequently by the sweat of anguish. One chilly November morning a sailor was walking down the Highway. His step was jerky and uncertain, for his feet were bare; his sole articles of dress consisted of a cotton shirt and a pair of trousers that seemed large enough to take another person inside of them. These were kept from dropping off by what is known as a soul-and-body lashing—that is, a piece of cord or rope-yarn tied round the waist. His manner indicated that he felt satisfied with himself and at peace with all creation, as he chanted with a husky voice the following song:—

"Sing goodbye to Sally, and goodbye to Sue;
Away—Rio!
And you who are listening, goodbye to you,
For we're bound to Rio Grande!
And away—Rio, aye Rio!
Sing fare ye well, my bonny young girl,
We're bound for Rio Grande!"

He was met by a shipmate just then who had been searching for him during several days. The song was cut short by the mutual warmth of greeting.

"What ho, Jack!" interjected the faithful comrade, with a gigantic laugh; "you are under very small canvas this morning. Have you been in heavy weather?"

"Yes," said Jack, "I have; but there's a fellow coming up astern must have had it worse than me. He *was* under bare poles, but I see he's got a suit of newspapers bent now, and he's forging ahead very fast!"

There is a grim humour about this story which brings a certain type of sailor vividly to mind.

CHAPTER XIII

THE MATTER-OF-FACT SAILOR

I always feel inclined to break the law when I see a West End or any other dandy on a theatrical stage libelling the sailor by his silly personification: hitching his breeches, slapping his thigh, lurching his body, and stalking about in a generally ludicrous fashion, at the same time using phrases which the real sailor would disdain to use: such as "my hearty," "shiver-my-timbers," and other stupid expressions that Jack of to-day never thinks of giving utterance to. If theatrical folk would only take the trouble to acquaint themselves with the real characteristics of the sailor, and caricature him accurately, they would find, even in these days, precious material to make play from. Even Jack's culpable vagaries, if reproduced in anything like original form, might be utilised to entertaining effect; but the professional person insists upon making him appear with a quid rolling about in his mouth and his stomach brimful of slang, which he empties as occasion may require. It may or may not go down with their audiences, but the tar himself cannot stand it. I was seated beside a typical sailor in a London theatre not very long ago, and a few gentlemen in nautical attire came one after the other strutting on to the stage. Their performances were quite unsailorly, so much so that my neighbour said to me: "If this goes on much longer I shall have to go. Just fancy," said he, "a matter-of-fact sailor making such a d——fool of himself!" I reminded him that this achievement was not so rare an occurrence. But he was not to be appeased! The sailor of the olden times never used tinsel nautical terms. His dialect was straight and strong, and his peculiar dandyism very funny. His hair used to be combed behind his ears, he wore a broad, flat cap cocked to one side, and his ears were adorned with light drops of gold or silver; and when he went forth to do his courting he seemed to be vastly puzzled as to the form his walk should take. Alas! all this has passed away, and our eyes shall see it never more; but the fascination of it is fixed in one's memory, and it is pleasant to think of even now.

The average seaman has always expressed himself with unmistakable clearness on matters pertaining to his profession. I was walking down the main street of a seafaring town some years ago, when I saw a group of people standing at a window looking at an oil-painting of a large, square-rigged ship which had been caught in a squall. The royals and top-gallant sails had been let fly, and they were supposed to be flapping about as sails will in a squall if the yards are not trimmed so as to keep them quiet. There were two sailors in the group who were criticising the painting with some warmth: the ropes were not as they should be, the braces and stays were not properly regulated, and "Whoever saw sails flying about like that!" said the more voluble of the two. The other dryly retorted, "I don't know, mister, what *you* think, but I want to say that I have seen them cut some d—— funny capers at times!" This very sailor-like sally both tickled the audience and convinced it that the sails were really correctly drawn.

On another occasion, during the prevalence of one of the most terrible easterly gales that ever visited the northeast coast, a multitude of people had congregated on the south pier at the mouth of the Tyne to witness the vessels making for the great Northern Harbour. The sight was awful in its peculiar beauty, the foam fluted and danced on the troubled air until it found a resting place far up the inner reaches of the harbour. There were seen in the distance two sailing vessels labouring amid a wrathful commotion of roaring seas. As they approached the harbour the excitement became universal. Women stood there transfixed with dread lest the storm-tossed vessels should be conveying some of their beloved relations to a tragic doom. Two gentlemen of clerical voice and appearance conversed with obvious agitation, one of whom audibly spoke of the grandeur and picturesque charm of the flurry of wild waters. "Look at them," said he, "as they curtsey and rustle along to the kiss of the tempest. Oh, it is a magnificent sight!"

A few burly, weather-beaten sailors stood hard by. It soon became apparent that their professional pride had been touched by the poetic babble to which they had listened. One of them took upon himself the task of interjecting what the practical opinion of himself and friends was by addressing the aesthetic dreamer in accents of stern reproof: "*You*," said he, "may call it grandeur and picturesque and magnificent and curt-seying, but we call it a damned dirty business. If you were aboard of one of them, you wouldn't talk about rustling through the cloven sea to the kiss of the tempest, you would be too tarnation keen on getting ashore!"

The orator had just finished his harangue when one of the vessels, a brigantine, was crossing the bar. The supreme moment had come. All eyes and minds were fixed on the doomed vessel; men were seen clinging to the rigging, and one solitary figure stood at the wheel directing her course through a field of rushing whiteness. She was supposed to have crossed the worst spot, when a terrific mountain of remorseless liquid was seen galloping with mad pace until it lashed over her and she became reduced to atoms. Nothing but wreckage was seen afterwards. The crew all perished. It was a heartrending sight, which sent the onlookers into uncontrollable grief. The sailor was right: "It was a dirty business."

The sporting instinct in the *bonâ-fide* British seaman was always very strong. The white-washed Yankee—that is to say, not a real American, but a Blue-nose, *i.e.*, a Nova Scotiaman—was never very popular, because of his traditional bullying and swaggering when all was going well, and his cowardice in times of danger. Once a vessel was coming from 'Frisco, and when off Cape Horn she ran into an ice-berg which towered high above the sailors' heads. There was great commotion and imminent peril. A Blue-nose was chief mate, and he became panic-stricken, flopped on to his knees, and piteously appealed for Divine interposition to save them from untimely death. The second mate, who was a real John Bull, believed in work rather than prayer, at least so long as their position threatened sudden extinction. He observed the petitioner in the undignified position of kneeling in prayer beside the mainmast. It angered him so that he put a peremptory stop to his pleadings by bringing his foot violently in contact with the posterior portion of his body, simultaneously asking him, "Why the h——- he did not pray before? It's not a damned bit of good praying now the trouble has arisen! Get on to your pins," said the irate officer, "and do some useful work! This is no time for snivelling lamentations. Keep the men in heart!" There was pretty fair logic in this rugged outburst of enlightenment. But while this striking flow of opposition to prayer under such circumstances was proceeding, the thought of peril was briefly obscured by the sight of a pretty little girl, a daughter of one of the passengers, frollicking with the ice which had tumbled on the deck, in innocent oblivion of the danger that encompassed her. What a beautiful picture! By skilful manoeuvring the vessel was extricated from an ugly position, and the unhappy first mate who had neglected to put himself into communication with the Deity before the accident happened, became the object of poignant dislike for having broken one of the most important articles of nautical faith by doing so afterwards!

CHAPTER XIV

RESOURCEFULNESS AND SHIPWRECK

If the oceans of the world could speak, what marvellous tales of heroism they could relate that are hidden in the oblivion of their depths. Sailors generally are singularly reticent about their adventures. They are sensitive about being thought boastful; the nature of their training and employment is so pregnant with danger that they become accustomed to treat what most people would consider very daring acts as a part of their ordinary business that should not be made a fuss about. Hence many a gallant deed has been done that was never heard of beyond the ocean and the

vessel where it took place.

There is not a crew that sails on salt water that could not relate after every voyage they make events and doings thrilling with interest which would be considered stirring and brave if they had taken place on shore among persons other than sailors. It is no uncommon thing to hear the cry "A man overboard!" while a vessel is being rushed through a heavy sea at a great speed, and the alarm is no sooner given than some gallant fellow is seen to jump overboard to his rescue. Not long ago a large vessel bound out to the west coast of South America was running before heavy north-east trade winds and a high following roller. A man was seen to fall from the foretopsail yard right overboard before the order could be given to haul the vessel to the wind. One of his shipmates plunged into the bosom of a mountainous sea without divesting himself of any clothing; even his boots had to be taken off in the water. The ship was promptly brought to the wind, and skilfully manipulated towards the drowning man and his rescuer. The order was given to lower the cutter, and a scramble was made for the distinction of being one of the crew. The two men battled with the waves until the boat reached them. They were taken into her and saved. A short paragraph in the newspapers telling the simple story was all that was heard of it.

Three years ago, Mr. Barney Barnato, the millionaire, was coming home from South Africa, and when off the Western Islands, from some cause or other he fell overboard. The mail steamer must have been going sixteen or seventeen knots an hour at the time, but it did not prevent the second officer (I think it was) from jumping in after him and recovering his body, though, alas! it was inanimate. This brave fellow's act was made famous by a gifted and wealthy young lady passenger falling in love with him, and he of course with her. They have since been married, and I wish them all the blessings that earth and heaven can bestow upon them. I believe Mrs. Barnato and the executors of the genial Barney showed their appreci-

ation in a suitable way also.

Few people except sailors and passengers who may have witnessed it can fully realise how difficult it must be to keep an eye on a person in the sea, even if it is perfectly smooth. It is one of the most exciting experiences of sea-life. All except the rescuing party and the man at the wheel run up the rigging and gaze with frantic eagerness to keep in view and direct the boat towards where they think the object of their mission is. It often happens that all their efforts are unavailing, and when the search has to be given up a creepy sensation, like some shuddering hint of death, takes possession of you. I have more than once felt it. Sailors on these occasions are subdued and divinely sentimental, though their courage remains undaunted.

There are, however, phases of bravery, endurance, and resourcefulness that test every fibre of the seaman's versatile composition; and a communication to the outer world of the tremendous struggles he is called upon to bear would be calculated to stagger the lay imagination. It would take a spacious library to contain all that could be written of his bitter experiences and toilsome pilgrimages throughout ages of storm and stress. The pity is so much of it is lost to us, but this again is owing to the sailor's habitual reticence about his own career. A characteristic instance of this occurred to me about six months ago. I had business in a shipyard, and the gateman who admitted me is one of the last of the seamen of the middle of the century. He was for many years master of sailing vessels belonging to a north-east coast port. He is a fine-looking, intelligent old fellow. I knew him by repute in my boyhood days; he had the reputation then of being a smart captain, and owners readily gave him employment. After greeting me with sailor-like cordiality, he commenced to converse about the old days, and as the conversation proceeded the weird sadness of his look gradually disappeared, his eyes began to sparkle, and joy soon suffused his ruddy face. His soul was ablaze with reminiscences, and his unaffected talk was easy and delightful to listen to. I was reluctant to break the charm of it by introducing a subject that might be distasteful to him. It was my desire to hear *from his own lips* a tale of shipwreck which is virtually without parallel in its ghastly tragedy. I instinctively felt myself creeping on to sacred ground. As soon as I mentioned the matter his countenance changed and he became pensive. A far-off look came over him, which indicated that a tender chord had been touched. Obviously his thoughts were revisiting the scene of a fierce conflict for life. The sight was sublime, and when I saw the moisture come into his eyes and his breast heave with emotion, it made me wish that I had not reminded him of it. At length he began to unfold the awful story. He was master of a brig called the *Ocean Queen*. I think he said it was in the month of December, 1874. They sailed from a Gulf of Finland port laden with deals. After many days they reached the longitude of Gotland; they were then overtaken by a hurricane from the west which battered the vessel until she became water-logged and dismasted. The crew lashed themselves where they could, and huddled together for warmth to minimise the effects of the biting frost and the mad turmoil of boiling foam which continuously swept over the doomed vessel, and caked itself into granite-like lumps of ice. At intervals they would try to keep their blood from freezing by watching a "slant" when there was a comparative smooth, and run along the deckload a few times, keeping hold of the life-line that was stretched fore and aft for this purpose. After twelve hours the force of the tempest was broken, and they were able to take more exercise, but they were without food and water, and no succour came near them. They held stoutly out against the privations for two days, then one after another began to succumb to the combined ravages of cold, thirst, and hunger. Some of them died insane, and others fought on until Nature became exhausted, and they also passed into the Valley of Death. There were now only the captain and a coloured seaman left. The wind and sea were

drifting the vessel towards the Prussian coast, and on the fifth morning after she became water-logged the wreck stranded on a sandy beach two hours before daylight. The captain and his coloured companion attached themselves to a plank, and by superhuman effort reached the shore. They buried their bodies up to the waist in sand under the shelter of a hill, believing it would generate some warmth into their impoverished systems. Their extremities were badly frostbitten, and when they were discovered at daylight by a man on horseback who had been attracted to the scene of the wreck, they were both in a condition of semi-consciousness. He galloped off for assistance, and speedily had them placed under medical treatment, and under the roof of hospitable people. A few days' rest and proper attention made them well enough to be removed to a hospital. It was soon found necessary to amputate both of the coloured man's legs, and also some of his fingers. The captain had the soles of his feet cut off; and he told me that he always regretted not having the feet taken off altogether, as he had never been free from suffering during all these years. He said the doctor advised it, but that he himself was so anxious to save them that he preferred to have the soles scraped to the bone, hoping that the diseased parts would heal; "but," said he with an air of sober melancholy, "they never have."

Long before this story of piercing sadness, and horror, and heroism, and superb endurance was finished, I felt a big lump in my throat, and every nerve of me was tingling with emotion; and as I passed from the presence of this noble old fellow and pondered over all he had so reluctantly and modestly told me of himself, it made me conclude that I had been holding converse with a hero! I have been obliged to confine myself to a brief outline of this tale of shipwreck. There are incidents of it too painful to relate, and I am quite sure I am consulting the wishes of the narrator by abstaining from going too minutely into detail. The main facts are given, and they may be relied on as absolutely true.

The seamen of the middle of the nineteenth century were trained to be ingenious and resourceful in emergencies, and, as a rule, they did not disgrace their training. If a jib-boom was carried away, a mast sprung, or a yard fractured, they had only to be told to have it fished. They knew how to do this as well as their officers did, and would not brook being instructed. If a mast was carried away they regarded it as a privilege to obey the captain's instructions to have jury masts rigged, and it is not an exaggeration to say that astonishing feats of genius have been done on occasions such as these.

In 1864 I was an apprentice aboard a brig bound from the Tyne to the Baltic; Tynemouth Castle bore west 60 miles. A strong north-west wind was blowing, and the sea was very cross. A press of canvas was being carried. The second mate being in charge, orders were given to take in the foretopgallant sail. It was clewed up, and just as another apprentice and myself were getting into the rigging to go up and furl it one of the chain-plates of the maintopmast backstays carried away. The maintopmast immediately snapped and went over the side, dragging the foretopmast with it. Fortunately we had not as yet got aloft, or we would have come to a precipitate end. The storm was increasing, and the confusion of ropes, chains, sails, spars, &c, all lurching against the side, caused the captain and his crew much concern, lest the vessel should be so injured as to endanger her safety. The men worked like Trojans to minimise danger, and to save as much gear as possible to rig jury masts with. The accident happened at 6 a.m., and at 8 p.m. the wreck had been cleared away and all the necessary gear saved. Over and over again during that toilsome day men risked their lives to save a few pounds' worth of gear; indeed, it was a day of brave deeds. On the following days it blew a hard northerly gale so that the vessel had to be hove-to. After that it gradually fined down, and the task of rigging jury topmasts began. It took four days to accomplish all that was necessary; and, although the men were fagged, they were also proud of their work. Any adverse criticism would have been visited with rigorous penalties. They were not boastful about it, though they quite believed a smart job had been carried out; and perhaps they took some credit to themselves for saving the vessel from total destruction. I have reason to know that neither the owner nor his underwriters estimated their services as being worthy of any recognition whatever. It was a custom in those days to guard strictly against the sin of generosity, even to recompense brave deeds done or valuable services rendered!

A fine clipper barque in those old days, one that was originally built for the tea trade, and had made many successful passages with that cargo from China to London, acquired an enviable reputation for her sailing qualities, but, like many others, she was driven out of the trade by the introduction of steam and more modern methods of transit. She, however, still continued to make for her owners large profits in the West Indian and American trades. In 1873 freights were very good out and home from the higher Baltic ports, and the owner decided to make a short voyage in that direction before resuming the West Indian employment. She had made a rapid passage from the Tyne, and was sailing along the island of Gotland with a strong northerly wind. The season was far advanced, and the captain was carrying a press of canvas which made her plunge along at the rate of at least twelve knots an hour. The captain, who had been on deck nearly the whole passage, set the course, and gave strict instructions to the second mate, whom he left in charge, to keep a sharp look-out while he was below having a wash.

It was 8 p.m.; the moon was just coming from below a hazy horizon, which made it difficult to see anything under sail except at a short distance. The lookout suddenly reported a vessel under sail right ahead without lights. The helm of the barque was starboarded; but it was too late. The vessel, which proved to be a brig, struck and raked along the starboard side, carrying away nearly the whole of the fore, main, and mizzen rigging, irreparably damaging some important sails. As soon as it was discovered that the colliding vessel had suffered no material damage, the captain gave orders for the vessel to be put on her course, and to unbend the torn sails and bend a fresh set before starting to secure the lee rigging, so that as little time as possible might be lost. While this was being done a minute survey was being made by the captain and the carpenter to ascertain the extent of the damage to rigging, chain-plates, and hull. It was found that the latter was uninjured; but the shrouds and chain-plates were badly damaged, especially the latter, and the only way of securing the rigging thoroughly was to heave-to for a while and pass two bights of hawser chain under the bottom so that some of the starboard fore and main rigging could be set up to it. This was soon done, and the barque put on her course once more. The men worked with commendable skill and energy during the whole night, and when the livid grey of the dawn came they had all but finished their arduous task. Fortunately the wind kept steady on the port beam, so that the damage to the starboard rigging could be secured without interrupting the progress of the voyage, it being on the leeside. At 9 a.m. the watches were again resumed, and those whose duty it was to be on deck proceeded to carry out the finishing touches. These were satisfactorily completed, and by the time the evening shadows had fallen the temporary repairs were closely scrutinised and pronounced so strong that no gale could destroy them. The moaning of the hoarse wind through the rigging, and the sinister appearance of the lowering clouds as they hurried away to leeward, indicated that mischief was in the air, and that there was every probability of the soundness of the renovated rigging being promptly tested. The wind and sea were making, with swift roaring anger, but not a stitch of canvas was taken in, every spar and rope-yarn aboard was feeling the strain as the clipper was crashed into the surging waves which flowed between the shores of an iron-bound gulf. The vessel was swept with exciting rapidity towards her destination, but before morning dawned the gale had become so fierce sail was ordered to be shortened. Soon the course had to be altered, and the full weight of the tempest was thrown on the damaged parts. The crew had the encouraging satisfaction of seeing that their hastily accomplished work refused to yield to the vast strain it was suddenly called upon to bear. They arrived at their discharging port without further mishap, and, with the exception of fitting new chain-plates to connect the shrouds to, everything else was secured by the crew, and she was brought home without incurring any further cost to her owners and underwriters. A very profitable voyage was made, and the captain had the distinction of receiving a condescending benediction from the manager on his arrival home. He was told with an air of unequalled majesty that in many ways the mishap was disastrous, "but," said the manager, "I am impelled to confess that it is atoned for by the singular display of merit which has been shown in not only extricating your vessel from a perilous position, but for your expedition and economy in carrying out the repairs!" The captain responded to this eloquent tribute by assuring his employer that he was deeply grateful for this further token of his confidence, and very shortly after he was materially rewarded from quite an unexpected source by being offered the command of a fine steamer, which he only accepted after considerable pressure had been brought to bear on him by the owners of the steamer and his own friends.

A BERWICKSHIRE HAVEN

Long before steamers had captured the coasting trade of the northern coal ports, a brig which carried coal from the Tyne, Blyth, or Amble to Calais, was caught by a terrific gale from the east when returning north in ballast. She managed to scrape round all the points until Coquet Island was reached, when it became apparent from the shore that it would be a miracle if she weathered the rocks which surround that picturesque islet. Her movements had been watched from the time she passed Newbiggin Point, and grave fears for her safety spread along the coast. The Coquet was closely shaved, but she was driven ashore between Alnmouth and Warkworth Harbour. The position was excitingly critical. It was low tide, and the storm raged with malignant force, so that when the flood made there seemed little hope of saving the crew. As to the vessel herself, it was only a question of time until she would be shattered into fragments.

A large crowd of people had congregated as near to the wreck as it was prudent, for the waves swept far up the beach. The crew sought refuge in the forerigging, as heavy seas were sweeping right over the hull, and as no succour came to them one brave fellow made a small line fast to his waist, and sprang into the cauldron of boiling breakers. He reached the shore almost lifeless, and his gallant act was the means of saving several of the crew, who dared to risk being hauled through the surf. Alas! as often happens, some of them still clung to the rigging that held the oscillating mast. It was assumed that they must be benumbed, or that they dreaded being dashed to death in the attempt to attach themselves to the rope that had been the means of rescuing their shipmates. The people gesticulated directions for them to take the plunge, but it seemed as though they were riveted to a tragic destiny.

Darkness had come on, and some one in the crowd shouted at the top of his voice, "Silence! I hear some one shouting." Instantly there was a deathlike hush, and mingling with the hurricane music of the storm, the sweet feminine voice which was said to be that of the cabin-boy was heard singing—
"Jesu, lover of my soul
Let me to Thy bosom fly,
While the nearer waters roll,
While the tempest still is high.
Hide me, oh my Saviour, hide,
Till the storm of life be past,
Safe into the haven guide,
Oh receive my soul at last."
These sentences came tossing through the troubled darkness, and when the last strains had faded away the subdued anguish of the people was let loose. Women became hysterical, and strong men were smitten with grief. It was a soul-stirring experience to them; and their impotence to save the perishing men was an unbearable agony. A shriek from some of the crowd told that something dreadful had happened. All eyes were directed towards the wreck, but nothing could be seen now but a portion of the half-submerged hull. The masts had gone by the board, and soon the coast was strewn with wreckage; she had broken all to pieces. When daylight broke, a search-party found the little songster's cold, clammy body. They wiped the yellow sand from his eyes and closed them, and in the course of the day his fellow-victims were laid at rest beside him.

CHAPTER XV

MANNING THE SERVICE

At the present time there is much writing and talking as to how the merchant service is to be kept supplied with seamen. Guilds, Navy Leagues, and other agencies of talk have been set at work to solve what they term a problem. Theories that are exasperating to read or listen to have been indiscriminately forced upon an enduring public; and after all the balderdash and jeremiads that have flowed copiously over the land we are pretty much where we were. The modern shipowner and his theoretic friends prefer to waste their energy in concocting theories to solve an imaginary problem—the only problem being that which exists in their own minds. There is nothing else to solve. Once the mildew is out of the way and the doors are set wide open, we shall soon have a full supply of recruits. During the last few years several steamship owners have so far overcome their prejudices as to take apprentices. Those who have worked it properly have succeeded; while others complain of the system being absolutely unsuccessful. My own impression is that the want of success is not the fault of the lads, but those who have the controlling of them.

Mr. Ritchie, when he was the head of the Board of Trade, introduced a system of barter, whereby a certain reduction of light dues was to be made to the firms who undertook to train boys for the merchant service and the Royal Naval Reserve. Needless to say, the very nature of the conditions caused it to fail. In the first place the parents of the boys looked upon the proposal as a form of conscription; and in the second, owners would have no truck with a partial abatement of the light dues. They very properly claimed that the charge should be abolished altogether. All other countries, except America and Turkey, have made the lighting of their coast-lines an Imperial question; and America only levies it against British shipping as a retaliatory measure. Mr. Ritchie lost his chance of doing a national service by neglecting to take into his confidence shipowners who were conversant with the voluntary system of training seamen. Had he done this, it is pretty certain they would have guided him clear of the difficulties he got into, and his measure would have been fashioned into a beneficent, workable scheme instead of proving a fiasco.

There are shipowners who believe that it is the duty of the State to pay a subsidy of twenty to fifty pounds per annum for every apprentice carried. I have always been puzzled to know from whence they derive their belief. When pressed to state definitely what arguments they have to give in favour of such a demand, their mental processes seem to become confused. They are driven to prophetic allusions to future naval war, and the usefulness of seamen in that event. Of course no one can dispute the usefulness of sailors at any time and under any circumstances; but if that is the only reason for asking the Government to pay owners part of the cost of manning their ships, then they are living in a fool's paradise, and are much too credulous about public philanthropy, and very unobservant and illogical too if they imagine that national interests are entirely centred in the industry they happen to be engaged in. It would be just as reasonable for Armstrong's or Vickers' to request a subsidy for training their men because their business happens to be the manufacture of guns and the construction of warships. Or on the same logical grounds the ordinary shipbuilder and engine-maker would be justified in cadging subsidies for training every branch of their trades, and thereby work their concerns at the expense of a public who are not directly connected with them. But no one has ever heard of these people making any such demand on national generosity. I believe I am right in stating that there are only very few shipowners who advocate such a parochial view. The great bulk of them regard it with disfavour, first, because it smacks of peddling dealing; and, secondly, even if it were right they know that State aid means State interference, and State interference savours too much of working commerce on strictly algebraic lines, which only an executive with a wealthy, indulgent nation behind it could stand. The Chamber of Shipping last year vigorously declared against subsidies of this kind; and the way in which the proposal was strangled leaves small hope of it ever being successfully revived.

An encouraging feature of the situation is that the Shipping Federation has at last taken the matter up. The late Mr. George Laws was always in favour of doing so, but unfortunately he got scant support from his members. Since his death, and the pronouncement the Chamber of Shipping gave in its favour at the last annual meeting, Mr. Cuthbert Laws, who succeeded his gifted father, has with commendable energy and marked ability undertaken the task of reviving the old system of every vessel carrying so many apprentices. He is

penetrating every part of Great Britain with the information that the Federated Shipowners are prepared to give suitable respectable lads of the poor and middle class a chance to enter the merchant service on terms of which even the poorest boy can avail himself, without pecuniary disability; and I wish the able young manager of the most powerful trade combination in the world all the success he deserves in his effort, not only to keep up the supply of seamen, but to raise the standard of the mercantile marine.

In the early years of the last century, right up to the seventies, north-country owners placed three to four apprentices on each vessel, and never less than three. Many of them came from Scotland, Shetland, Norfolk, Denmark and Sweden. There were few desertions, and they always settled down in the port that they served their time from. If any attempt was made at engaging what was known as a "half-marrow" [2] there was rebellion at once; and I have known instances where lads positively refused to sail in a vessel where one of these had been shipped instead of an apprentice. Impertinent intrusion was never permitted in those days. As soon as they were out of their time the majority of the lads joined the local union. One of the conditions of membership was that each applicant should pass an examination in seamanship before a committee of the finest sailors in the world. They had to know how to put a clew into a square and fore-and-aft sail, to turn up a shroud, to make every conceivable knot and splice, to graft a bucket-rope, and to fit a mast cover. The examination was no sham. I remember one poor fellow, who had served five years, was refused membership because he had failed to comply with some of the rules. He had to serve two years more before he was admitted. I have often regretted that Mr. Havelock Wilson did not adopt similar methods for his union, though perhaps it is scarcely fair to put the responsibility of not doing so on him. The conditions under which he formed his union were vastly different from what they were in those days. He had to deal with a huge

disorganised, moving mass, composed of many nationalities. At the same time I am convinced that a union conducted on the plan of the one I have been describing is capable of doing much towards training an efficient race of seamen, and I hope Mr. Wilson, or somebody else, will give it a trial.

Since the above was written Lord Brassey, by the invitation of the Newcastle Chamber of Commerce, has read a carefully prepared paper, in the Guildhall, to a large audience of shipowners and merchants, on the best means of feeding the Mercantile Marine and the Royal Navy with seamen. Lord Brassey must have been at infinite trouble in getting the material for his paper, and, notwithstanding the errors of fact and of reasoning in it, I think the shipping community, and indeed the public at large, owe him their hearty thanks for giving so important a subject an opportunity of being discussed. So far as his advocacy of the establishment of training vessels for the supply of seamen to the Royal Navy is concerned, I have nothing to say against it. The lads in those ships are trained by naval officers, under naval customs and discipline, and there should be some recruiting ground of the kind for that service. But Lord Brassey advocates it for the Mercantile Marine also. He suggests a plan of subsidy to be paid to the owner or the apprentice, and that the lad after serving four years, should be available for service in the Royal Navy. But to begin with, it may be objected that men trained in Royal Navy discipline and habits never mix well with men trained in the other service; their customs and habits of life and work are quite different to those of the merchant seaman. It used to be a recognised belief that the sailor of the merchantman could adapt himself with striking facility to the work of the Royal Navy and its discipline, but the Navy trained man was never successful aboard a cargo vessel. The former impression originated, no doubt, during the good old times when it was customary for prowling ruffians from men-of-war to drag harmless British citizens from their homes to man H.M.

Navy, and all the world knows how quickly they adapted themselves to new conditions, and how well they fought British battles! But what a sickening reality to ponder over, that less than a century ago the powerful caste in this country were permitted, in defiance of law, to have press-gangs formed for the purpose of kidnapping respectable seamen into a service that was made at that time a barbarous despotism by a set of brainless whipper-snappers who gained their rank by backstair intrigue with a shameless aristocracy! All that kind of villainy has been wiped out; and the men of the Royal Navy are now treated like human beings; and they do their work not a whit less courageously and well than they did when it was customary to lash God's creatures with strands of whipcord loaded with lead until the blood oozed from their skins. There is no need to press either men or boys to enter the King's Naval Service. It has now been made sufficiently attractive to obviate the need for that. Nor is there any necessity for shipowners to be called upon, with or without subsidy, to train and supply men for the Navy. They have enough to do to look after their own manning, and this can be done easily by the adoption of methods that will break down any objection British parents may have to their sons becoming indentured to steamship owners, who will find work for them to do, and who will have

them trained by a kindly discipline, paid, fed, and lodged properly; but still, if they are to be thorough men, there should be no pampering. Unquestionably, then, the place for training should be aboard the vessels they are intended to man and become officers and masters of. No need for subsidised training vessels; and certainly no need for a national charge being made for the benefit of shipowners, who have no right to expect that any part of their working expenses should be paid by the State.

As an example of how sympathy is growing for the apprenticeship system, Messrs. Watts, [3] Watts & Company, of London, have for many years carried apprentices aboard their steamers, and the grand old Blythman who adorns the City of London commercial life with all that is ruggedly honest and manly, has just purchased, at great cost, a place in Norfolk, which his generous son, Shadforth, has agreed to furnish, and then it is to be endowed as a training-field for sailor-boys. The veteran shipowner is well known by his many unostentatious acts of philanthropy to have as big a heart as ever swelled in a human breast; but, knowing him as I do, I feel assured that his philanthropy would have taken another form had he not been convinced he was conferring a real national benefit by giving larger opportunities to British lads to enter the merchant service.

I give two other notable examples of

success because of the care taken in selecting the boys and the care adopted in training them. Mr. Henry Radcliffe, senior partner of Messrs. Evan Thomas, Radcliffe & Co., of Cardiff, has taken a personal interest in boy apprentices for years. His experience of them has long passed the experimental state, and his testimony is that this is the only way the merchant navy can be adequately and efficiently maintained.

Daniel Stephens, senior partner of Messrs. Stephens, Sutton & Stephens, which firm has carried apprentices for a number of years, is a sailor himself, who has had the good sense never to try and hide the fact that he was trained amid a fine race of west-country seaman, and he is proud to be able to say that he has been training boys for years with uniform satisfaction. He relates with obvious pride that one of his boys, a coal-miner's son, seven years to a day from the date of joining his firm as an apprentice, sailed as chief officer of their newest and largest steamer.

FOOTNOTES:

[2] A "half-marrow" was a young man who was trying to become a seaman without serving his apprenticeship.

[3] During the passage of this book through the press, Mr. Watts, senior, has passed away.

Lightning Source UK Ltd.
Milton Keynes UK
UKOW05f0612290116

267377UK00007B/124/P